1.

Guardia Civil office, Villargordo del Cabriel, 23 June 1:01 CET

"I killed a man in Madrid." David Harris gazed blankly

as he confessed his crime to the salt-and-pepper-haired, hand-

some Spanish police officer, Javier Guaita. The sixty-something,

seasoned detective rocked back in his metal chair. When he had

escorted David into the interrogation room of the remote po-

lice station in the village of Villargordo del Cabriel, just outside

of Valencia, Spain, it had been silent. Nothing had stirred ex-

cept the shuffling of their feet as they entered — the sand from

the desert outside scraped the floor beneath their shoes. It was

the kind of quiet only found in the post-midnight hours. An ambient buzz from the cicadas and hum of the occasionally lone car speeding by on the highway several miles in the distance over the hot, arid terrain slowly drifted into the room. It only amplified the void. A bead of sweat appeared on Jefe Inspector Guaita's forehead and slowly cascaded past his silvery brow, revealing the creases of age in his face down to his chiseled chin.

Unrestrained in the interrogation room, David's sleepless eyes stared at his reflection in the two-way mirror, past Guaita's confounded gaze. Javier's gentlemanly features were now morose.

The night silence had been broken.

Guaita had been annoyed by the unexpected call on this late summer evening. The young desk clerk attending the otherwise nearly-abandoned Guardia Civil outpost called Guaita in as he sipped on his fifth beer of the night, just as he was about to turn in. He wasn't supposed to drink while on duty, but nothing ever happened out here in this dusty, forgotten village. She had reported to Javier that a lost tourist came in on an expired visa and wanted help getting out of the country. It took him a few extra minutes to get to the station than normal —

he needed a little time to sober up. Driving the few kilometers over, he panned his eyes across the terrain and wondered what in the world a tourist was doing in this part of Spain.

Led to believe that he was sitting across from a dumb, drunk American, the Inspector was bewildered by the confession. He recoiled and let the sobering moment settle in before responding. Diplomatically, Guaita repositioned, "Señor Smith. Por favor ... please. I do not have time for, eh ... jokes. It is very late. Let us discuss this from the start, ¿Sí? Señor David Smith, from Los Estados Unidos. Vamos a ver. Let us see."

Javier removed his reading glasses from his top breast shirt pocket. Looking down his nose, through the weathered spectacles at his notebook out of habit, he realized there was nothing to confer with. He was typically a diligent note-taker. The distraction of this American man disrupted his usual protocols and it had just occurred to Guaita through his inebriation that he had nothing to go on. His clerk was preoccupied with her social life and had given him no notes nor any intelligence. This was no investigation. This was just a lost tourist he was staring at. He had not even heard a report of a murder in Madrid. He usually heard the chatter if and when there was one. The low murder rates of the city, comparatively to the rest of the world's capitals, attract much attention and speculation.

Guaita continued under a facade of preparedness and control. "You asked me here on this Sunday evening because your three-month tourist visa expired, No? Dime. Tell me – why are you still here Señor Smith? What are you doing in this part of Spain? It is very remote. And, if you did lose your passport, why didn't you just go to the American Consulate while you were in Madrid?" asked the Inspector Jefe in his best, yet child-like English, unable to remove his thick, Valenciano accent. It had escaped Javier entirely why this man, and his name, seemed eerily familiar. Perhaps it was just the Ativan—taken to calm his mind from his service in Afghanistan with the Spanish

Armed Forces as a young man — mixed with the beers and earlier two glasses of his community's vineyard's vino tinto, playing tricks on his mind. Perhaps it was more than that.

"I am here because..." David replied in his mild Southern drawl, "Because, I killed a man in Madrid ... earlier tonight. His name ... his name was Raúl Garcia."

Javier's left eyebrow cocked. Slowly, his mouth gaped open.

David took the policeman's shocked pause to continue his methodical, planned confession in a casual cadence, "I never would've considered myself a killer. I mean, who thinks of themselves that way? I suppose, though, if I really thought about my life, maybe. Maybe my shortcomings, my frustrations, my mistakes ... I reckon there's something there," David looked down at the table and paused, shifting to portray melancholy.

David shook his head gently back and forth, looking down, appearing as in disbelief and swallowed the lump in his throat. His face lifted and he stared stoically at Javier, "It's funny though ... extinguishing another man's life wasn't the hardest thing I've ever had to do. But I did it, plain and simple. Ain't nothing much more to it. Things just turned out this way, and I can't take them back."

Stunned, the Inspector surveyed the room for assistance. Nothing aided his confusion. Only his antiquated walkie-talkie and his unused side arm holster rested on his aging hip. He nervously shuffled to make sure they were still there. Inspector Jefe Javier Guaita hadn't needed his firearm in many years. During the night shift, he was generally tasked with overseeing local traffic infractions and handling the occasional town drunkard when he was on duty. He had earned this late-night leisurely spot after 20 years in the Guardia. Though, he was preoccupied lately with his side employment, moonlighting as private security detail for a wealthy American pharmaceutical businessman and his Spanish-based operations. His police post with the Spanish Civil Guard, Spain's oldest countrywide police network, he kept merely as a formality and the occasional perk of having a badge.

Javier's hand discreetly searched for the security of his sidearm, finding only an empty holster. He unraveled with the thought of his unused gun sitting on his dresser at home currently. He replied, confounded and egregiously, now beginning to believe that David might be telling the truth, "¿Que? ¿Como? So ... eh ... you killed someone in Madrid? ¿Quien? Eh ... who? Who was this man you killed? Raúl ..."

Before David could respond, Guaita briefly and frantically uttered hasty, unintelligible Spanish into his walkie-talkie to the only other person in the building. That same young desk clerk sitting at an antiquated, mid-century desk at the front of the dilapidated building — she was the one who called Javier in at this late hour and was currently outside smoking and texting, away from her desk and the walkie. There was no response. After hours cops are hard to come by in this part of Spain. Javier Guaita was, effectively, alone. Still impatiently fidgeting and looking around for some sort of assistance, he continued his attempt at interrogation, befuddled at why this strange American was sitting across the table from him.

"Señor Smith, you contacted our office this evening to ask for assistance with exiting Spain on your expired visa. Pero ... but, you are confessing to a ... a murder?" Javier's lack of comprehension and now distorted facial expressions irritated David.

"If that's what you would prefer to call it, yes." David continued calmly, "I will tell you everything you need to know. Please ... take your time, collect your thoughts and grab a pen and paper if you prefer."

Standing up from the table Guaita stepped back, "I, I ... you must permit me un momento, Señor Smith." A visibly bewildered Guaita continued, pointing at David in a fatherly manner, "I need to make a phone call."

As the Inspector Jefe hastily left the room, he began dialing a number on his cell phone. David heard muffled, angry tones through the cracked door. He angrily whispered into his phone for 10 seconds, walked across the hall and stomped back to the room. David could hear everything echoing in this old building. David chewed at his finger nails that were now leaking blood from his incessant habit. He paused to feel for the weapon concealed in his back. David carefully considered his next words to the inspector. A buzz from the fluorescent light overhead crackled. David reminded himself of why he was here and why he specifically called Inspector Guaita personally. David knew Javier would be the one to meet him here on this dark, late night. Javier Guaita was the man he needed.

The door swung open abruptly. Javier attempted to regain control of the unraveling affair. Unprepared, Inspector Guaita had no idea what he was going to do with this man. He had no backup, no weapon and no restraints. He hadn't even considered the need for them until he made his way to the chair opposite David once again. Off-guard and flustered, he failed to check the trunk of his car or the rest of the station for munitions.

"Puta Madre," he spurted.

In the blurry, buzzed exit from his villa home on that late evening for what was supposed to be a simple conversation with a confused, stupid tourist, Guaita realized he had made too many mistakes to do anything other than let this man tell the rest of his story.

"You, you don't move, comprendes? Finish your story," Guaita demanded, pointing at David's face and then pointing his finger downward to the cold, steel table. The table reminded David of the events that led him to this encounter and he became renewed with purpose. David knew they were still alone, aside from the young front desk clerk who wasn't paid enough to be working there this late and had taken a break from her post when they first entered the building. Guaita sat down across from David. The two men were now sweating together in the stifling room.

"Where were we, Señor Smith? Por favor, please tell me everything, todo," Guaita waved his hands, emphasizing his requirement for David to tell the whole story from the beginning. He jostled into his seat, recalibrated his attitude and crossed his arms authoritatively.

David Harris complied happily, "I made a choice, you see? I had to do it. I was always meant to be a part of this … this nasty business. Course, took me some time to realize that I was a killer. That I had that in me, you know?" David paused, cocked his head at the officer, looked at himself in the mirror, then continued, "As I said, the man's name was Raúl Garcia. I was in a bar, there, in Madrid. I believe it was in the La Latina neighborhood. A bar called El Schotis. You know the one, no? The one that the politicians and businessmen like to frequent. It's a popular joint."

No verbal response from Guaita. His wild, racing eyes gave away his position.

David ran his fingers through his wavy, dark brown hair, "Well, he was there, drinking cañas, stuffing his greasy, fat face with patatas bravas and olives stuffed with anchovies. He had a shortly trimmed beard, thick black hair, deep set brown eyes and bushy eyebrows."

For a moment, David paused, remembering that night and that there was almost a teddy bear-like quality to Raúl's features. He could tell that earlier on in his life he may have been somewhat fit, judging by his tailored short sleeve dress shirt that boasted strong arms. Yet, they were overshadowed by his bulging belly, no doubt a result of his ravenous consumption of pinchos, cañas and a generally leisurely existence. He also seemed out of place here at this particular bar, as if he was reaching for the next class. He forcibly entered conversations amongst the smaller circles of men. Laughing at jokes that he wasn't a part of. They still permitted his menacing presence.

"He stood there leaning casually against the marble bar amidst the smoke and rabble of that night's crowd, laughing with his friends. But come to think of it ... they didn't seem like friends. More like colleagues that tolerated him. I stood down the bar from him, trying to watch him only looking at him intermittently and quickly returning to my drink so as to not attract too much attention."

"So you were chasing, eh ... what is the word? Stalking ... this man, this Raúl Garcia?" The inspector inquired.

"I guess you could call it that, but I didn't know of this man until I decided to kill him. I found him and proceeded to follow him." David continued, "It was almost 11 p.m., and with it still being light out, I waited for him to get drunk and walk home."

"So," the inspector said, "you hunt your prey on La Noche de las Barbaras ... interesante. ¿Por que? Why? What did you do to this man? How did you kill him?" David knew that the Inspector was containing himself.

David continued the confession with robotic indifference, "After about another hour, Raúl took one last sip, said a few goodbyes, shoved off the spot on the bar he had been maintaining all evening and made his way out through the front entrance. Everyone was happy to see him go. I still had to pay for my drinks and tapas and shuffled into my pockets to find a few Euros. I had no time to wait for the bartender's attention, so I whistled, threw him a 10 and ran out the door after Raúl. If they had security cameras, I'm sure you could see me in there. Raúl had made it a few blocks walking briskly, smoking his Marlboro Reds and glancing over his left shoulder every few strides – it was almost as if he knew I was coming for him. I was actually envious of this man, envious that he was this fat and happy, wearing designer jeans, nice Italian shoes and a tailored shirt. I can't afford the clothes he was wearing."

"Señor Smith, this man, you killed him … to, to rob him?" The inspector asked with increasing frustration.

David continued undistracted, "He didn't see me but I was getting a little too close. I couldn't help it; I couldn't wait to plunge my knife into him. It was going to feel so good. You know?"

The inspector shuffled again uncomfortably in his seat, with a look of sickness in his face. Defiantly, he collected himself and stubbornly, pounded the table with his fist, "Please Señor, go on … tell me how you killed Señor Garcia."

David's thoughts drifted for a moment, going silent and recalling the last several hours. Las Noches Bárbaras was the longest day of the year in which the sunlight doesn't fade until almost midnight. It was a night conceived, in its earliest folk incantations, in order to scare the witches of Spain out of hiding and into the air, effectively banishing them to the night. It was a strange holiday for a country to celebrate that now mostly culminated in a festival of dance, music and art in Madrid. Not dissimilar to the bastardization of the All Hallows Eve holiday that became the American Halloween holiday. David had felt a familiar volatility in his heart that night, like he did as a mischievous child during *his* Halloweens. David stalked Raúl through the musty and smoke- and urine-filled streets, knowing that no one knew he existed right then and right there. He felt powerful and devious knowing that Garcia's life was in his hands. Feeling that rush of power following him, his heart raced wildly. But then he remembered his plaguing anguish. He was tormented by an uncontrollable rage that came flooding back. His purpose resolute, he slinked and slipped into empty doorways, leaning against centuries of grime and modern graffiti, oblivious to his generally obsessive nature to remain clean. The smells of sulfur, smoke, old beer and piss incensed his hatred only further for Garcia and for Spain. He had always hated Spain. He was insatiable on his quest and would not be quenched until he saw the light leave Garcia's eyes as he strangled it out of him. Garcia would be dead tonight.

"Por favor, David, go on," Guaita demanded emphatically interrupting David's glazed trance.

David continued to methodically recall the night, "I managed to follow him unnoticed through several blocks before reaching his flat. That's when he gave another look over his shoulder and walked in. I ran as fast as I could to catch the outer door to the stairs before it latched. I just barely caught it. Had it closed, I wouldn't of … well … maybe there was someone looking out for me. Anyway, I crept in very slowly and quietly so he wouldn't hear me. I think he knew someone was following him by then, though. There was no elevator and as I made my way up the stairs, I could hear him heaving throughout the stairwell a few flights above me. I waited for him to enter his apartment. I listened as he jangled his keys and fidgeted with the handle from a few stairs below, just out of view as he closed the door. I sat there for a few moments trying to plot a way to get him to open the door. The only thing I could think of was to try and intimidate him somehow, like the way a police officer would. It took me a minute, but I was convinced it would work. That's when I made my move. I held my hand over his peephole and yelled, "Policía!" and banged on the door repeatedly. He cracked it open and I slammed my foot into the door in the middle of the door; the force sent him stumbling back, but he regained his composure rather quickly for such a fat guy. Well, at any rate, he was shocked at my forceful intrusion. He was quick on the uptake though. He recoiled quickly into some kinda wrestler's grappling stance — I had never seen someone so ready for a fight that fast, quite honestly. I wasn't really ready for him to struggle. I hadn't worked that part out. I reckoned I would get the jump on him and stab him. But it didn't quite work out like that. I pulled out the knife that I was carrying with me…"

"Let me understand perfectly clear. You stalked Señor Raúl Garcia back to his flat and murdered him with your knife. This happened tonight? Is this correct Señor Smith?" The Inspector interrupted, pretending to jot notes into that weathered notebook.

Undeterred in his obtuse retelling, "Yes, as I was saying … I took out my knife, he lunged for me and we tumbled to the carpet."

David Harris continued, "He … he, started to beg for his life when I managed to get back on top of him. He pleaded with me, begging for the sake of his family with tears in his eyes starting to form. I really remember that part very distinctly. He was afraid. I soaked that moment up — it was just … just so satisfying. That's when I stuck my knife deep into his throat, retracting it only to stare into his eyes as the pain began to register in his brain. I gave him a moment, and then I slit across his throat, just below his chin … I don't … I don't think that I have ever seen that much blood before. It was a lot. Like, really a lot. It was like winning a jackpot in a slot machine — just flowing."

David's chilling candor entranced Javier, "Almost euphoric – you know? Indescribable, really. I watched the life leave his eyes. Have you ever done that? Have you ever held that much power over someone? It's … it's strange … but beautiful. You know, he looked peaceful, actually, once it was done and his body stopped squirming an' all."

Thoroughly disturbed, Guaita's stomach audibly churned. David paused and gave an aloof sniff through his nostrils as if to suggest he was proud of the endeavor. He shrugged off his cold-blooded killer confession and continued casually, as any sociopath would, "Anyway, I heard someone walking 'round outside and I began to clean up the mess. I washed my knife and hands and worked on getting his big body out of his apartment."

The Inspector was visibly nauseous, his terror palpable, "You will remain aquí, here in my custody, until I can verify this … this … story you tell me. We will call the authorities in Madrid. Tienes problemas. You are a disturbed man, Señor Smith." Nervously standing up, his hands trembled as he stood and walked around behind David to escort him to a holding cell.

"I have more to tell you Inspector; wouldn't you like to hear about what I did with the body? Wouldn't you like to know *why* I sliced Raúl Garcia from ear to ear?" David asked hoping to buy a little more time.

"I must lock you in one of our cells tonight and we will talk mañana once I have the chance to call…" Inspector Guaita replied.

"No, Señor Guaita that just won't do. That just won't do at all," David rebutted, standing up from his chair. Javier regretted leaving David unrestrained.

2.

Raúl Garcia dragged deeply on his cigarette, smoldered the remainder on the bottom of his Italian loafers and tucked it behind his ear as he observed the slender, attractive young American woman struggling to pull her roller luggage across the plaza. Though he is a larger, somewhat fat man, he cared about his appearance, or at least *his* perception of it, sparing no expense when it came to his wardrobe. He curated his inimitable sartorial appearance and was proud of the result. Anyone with a semblance of importance in this city knew exactly who Raúl Garcia was; at least that's what his own narcissism led him to believe. His appearance was everything. It especially upset him whenever blood spattered on those pricier tailored shirts he worked so hard for. It was difficult for a man of his stature to find clothing that flattered his shape. He was a man of distinguished taste, laboriously hunting the city for the finest fabrics and the most adept Korean tailors. His thick, black hair and chiseled chin lent themselves to his good looks but his crimes began to take their toll on his face. He had to accommodate for

his failing beauty and shape by elevating his wardrobe. His van-

ity was extravagant. He spent his recent earnings on good, qual-

ity clothing like those beautifully tailored shirts, wool or linen

blended slacks, exquisite Italian loafers, cocaine and, then of

course, there was the gambling. Luckily, his newest gig padded

his wallet a little more generously to pay for such things. He had

no real family to speak of to waste money on, and he was, more

than anything else, just a cold, methodical sociopath. There

was no discretion when it came to his victims – his killings were

merciless.

The street performer dressed in the knock-off Elmo costume that had been hassling tourists and their children in the
square in front of Garcia, stopped immediately and removed his
Elmo head the moment he noticed Garcia's presence, passing
by the young woman. The performer's hurried, sweaty-headed
exit puzzled the foreign children and pleased their parents. His
hasty retreat mirrored that of prey sensing an apex predator
nearby. Garcia proceeded behind the woman.

His expert trailing techniques, which he earned in the
Policia Municipal as an Officer before being fired for excessive
force a couple of years prior, eluded the woman as she made
her way through the narrow streets off of the square. Ham museums, Flamenco shows, cheap tourist accoutrements and cer-
vezerias adorned the streets closest to the square. Garcia's eye
momentarily flickered off of his prey as he caught two men
playing dice out of the corner of his eye. He struggled for a split
second but regained his focus, leaning against the stone wall of

the corner as the woman paused to look around at the stores. As the tourist trappings gave way on those narrow corridors, and opened up to the larger surface streets, beautiful trees filled the vista and lovely cafés bustled with attractive and smartly dressed patrons. The way the all-day sun bakes the concrete and marble on Madrid's streets and buildings makes any exposed surface hot enough to fry an egg on in the summer months. Misery is only relieved by finding shade this time of year. The little old ladies, with their dyed maroon and blue hair and their vintage, lacy dresses sought solace from the blaze of the fire ball above, scurrying to whatever side of the street the shade fell on. They knew their shady routes and stuck to them. Garcia, however, was used to the heat, even preferring it to the winter months. Blood is thinner, easier to clean off when it's hot out.

During his tenure as an Officer, he relished the physical violence he was able to project on supposed criminals. He asserted his position of power over the prostitutes that haunted the tourist areas between Plaza Mayor, Puerta del Sol and Gran Via, sexually assaulting them any time he felt a whim to do so. Those cravings usually came in the nighttime hours after losing his earnings in a card or dominoes game.

His peccadillos and penchants finally caught up with him when he nearly choked a murder suspect to death in a back alley one night after a particularly heavy loss in a card game of Botiffarra. He intended to coerce the suspect into confession but got carried away with the exuberant feeling. He loved doing it and bragged about it jokingly that it was in self-defense to his unwitting colleagues. And he looked forward to doing it again. That was, until the suspect's mother brought in her team of lawyers to petition against the police — the boy was released and Garcia was fired. There was never enough evidence to convict Garcia of the ordeal but the police force couldn't afford such a public relations disaster and letting him go was the only option.

During the time before getting hired as private security for a pharmaceutical research firm — thanks to his old pal in the Guardia Civil — he began killing. At first, it was a North African prostitute in Retiro Park. Then, a few more, just to make sure he liked it. They were just street urchins, petty thieves, punks, immigrants. Nobody missed them. Raúl, likewise, had no concessions to repress his appetite.

Today was a good day for Raúl. An advance payment from his newly acquired pharma client rested in an envelope at his flat, an easy target, and the opportunity to get that insatiable thrill from taking a life. Garcia watched the woman crossing Calle de Montalbán from the cover of a café adjacent to her as she got closer to her destination.

"It will never end, will it?" abruptly asked the attending waiter at the café in his Madrileño accent. Garcia disrupted from his concentration stared blankly in return at the stranger. "The heat. This heat is unbearable, no?" the kind Spaniard, just making conversation said. Garcia, disrupted from his stalking, disregarded him and hurriedly headed in the direction of the hotel, crossing to the shady side of the street.

The young woman took in the sights as she made this long walk to to the front desk of Petit Palace Savoy Alfonso XII hotel overlooking Parque Retiro on that hot, late morning. She never even looked over her shoulder. Raúl dually took notice of her distracted body language and assessed his prey.

Texting one of his young thugs while en route, he coordinated a meeting across from the hotel in the Parque Retiro. Meeting the eager, young street kid, the pair watched the American check in and enter the elevator from the shade of a tree across Calle de Alfonso XII. Knowing full well that bribery crosses a multitude of socioeconomic demographics in Madrid, Garcia had the kid slip the concierge at the hotel a €50 to discover the room number the young American woman had checked into and report back to him. As a former 19th century palace that had been converted into a chic, boutique hotel, the elegant exterior architecture and clean, modern interior invited savvy travelers and those looking for a calm reprieve from the boisterous city. Garcia's nefarious intentions starkly contrasted the safe and relaxing atmosphere as he made his way slyly past the concierge and up the marble stairs to the third floor. He never took the elevator, he was too discreet for that. The creaking floors on the third level under the weight of his hefty frame irritated Garcia, however. He pulled out his latex gloves.

Unaware, the young American woman washed her face in her bathroom as Garcia expertly and quietly picked the lock of room 308 with his small pocket knife. It was a cheap gift from his new employer that had their logo on it — it was the perfect size for discreetly picking locks. This private security gig for this pharma firm had many other perks aside from freebie marketing materials. Gaining entry unnoticed was one of Garcia's specialties; he was unnaturally nimble for his frame.

A sudden ring of the woman's cell phone startled Garcia into stealthily slipping undetected into the coat closet of the opulent room. The attractive woman turned off the running water and walked back to the room to retrieve it.

"Hi babe ... yes, I made it. I'm sorry I was going to call when I got off the plane, but I was shanghaied by some old lady who asked me to help her get her bags down from the overhead, and then the team was there to pick me up at the airport ... I just ... I just got caught off guard ... they wanted to welcome me. I got distracted, I'm sorry. Yes, I'm at the hotel now. I have dinner with Richard this evening and then meetings all day tomorrow. I promise I'll call first thing in the morning though. Okay, I love you too." She didn't want her husband to worry too much about what she had been up to between her arrival and ride to the hotel earlier that morning and why she really hadn't called.

Garcia listened for his opportunity to make his way back

out from behind the cracked closet door. He slid out, got up, grabbed the wire line from his pocket and quietly walked up behind the woman. Completely oblivious and preoccupied with her feverish typing on her phone, she pressed send on her final text message as Garcia made his final approach. He was graceful, gentle even. The young, beautiful woman was dead before she knew what was happening or that someone else was even in the room. In the blink of an eye, she was extinguished by the professional. Garcia made it quick to avoid a scuffle and draw any attention that any sort of struggle had occurred. He recognized this was a decent, lovely woman but despite the senselessness, he was getting paid a large sum. Her tucked-in poplin shirt, her navy pencil skirt and her high heels remained perfectly clothed on her freshly dead body. He took pride in knowing that he had taken her life silently, swiftly and almost painlessly. Sadness wanted to creep in but in an instant, his mania took over. He generally enjoyed watching others squirm and squeal for mercy but liked the fact that he took this young lady out in a kind way, sparing her much pain. He reaffirmed his mercy to himself as he sat down on the edge of the large bed.

Garcia picked up her phone that still remained unlocked and thumbed through a few of her photos, skipping over her messages. He couldn't resist. He needed to know more about her to encapsulate her as a trophy in his mind. She was married; several pictures of her and her husband on a beach and mountain scenes filled the gallery but the more recent pictures were mostly just selfies of her, dressed up, makeup on, heels on. Garcia pulled the paracord he had packed in his pocket out and tied a simple noose around the dead woman's neck. Utilizing the hotel's beautiful turn-of-the-century chandelier above the bed, he flung the cord over, stood on the bed and hoisted her up. He hung her body from it, dropped the note given to him to plant and closed the door behind him. He was out of the room as quickly as he had entered it. At the foot of the bed, Garcia's "Valencian Bioscience" emblazoned pocket knife laid, unclaimed, after falling out of his pocket during the operation.

"Es completo," Garcia typed into his own phone walking back down the marble stairs and into the dry, hot air. Looking around, he decided that he'd stroll under the lush, deciduous shade of Parque Retiro, have a cigarette and watch the ducks for a few minutes. They reminded him of his childhood. He used to come to this park as a boy with his father to feed the ducks. He wondered if these were from the same lineage. He took a drag, remembered his father and how he would crack him in the head when he came home drunk. And how this drunk father would rape his mother. Cirrhosis took his life from behind prison bars while Raúl was still young but not before he was able to strangle his mother to death. Raúl took another drag. He flicked his smoldering cigarette at the innocent ducks, hitting one and startling the flock. Raúl turned and walked away from the disrupted, squawking and flapping ducks.

Lovers canoodled on blankets, weary workers laid under trees and tourists traversed the lake on rented paddle boats. It was an exceptionally hot day now, but in the shade of the park, it was perfect. Garcia sprung for an ice cream at one of the handcart vendors — his father would never buy his fat little boy any ice cream. Raúl slowly savored the treat and decided that it was time for a new shirt. The foray with the young American woman left a faint bit of sweat and a hint of her perfume. For a moment, he flirted with the fantasy of a dalliance with her in his prime. He let it fade as a whiff of concern floated into his mind — that of DNA. Eh, he was clean, he thought; no one would find any of him in the hotel room. He paid it no further mind and recalibrated on the thought of a new shirt. Stripes? Gingham? No, too gauche and popular with the young men. He settled on a solid faint, light pink. It was summery and light but still conservative — a newer look he was trying to master to fit in with new friends.

Calle de Serrano was his favorite place to go shopping —

it featured the couture menswear stores that he couldn't afford prior to his new gig and it was a short walk away from the park. He nodded as he thought of the idea and happily made up his mind to head in that direction. Maybe he'll make his way over to Calle Fuencarrall afterward too, he thought. He loved the energy on that street; the fashion district drew in the hipsters, the fashionistas, the homosexuals – it made for great people watching. Sure, a decent walk from Serrano, but his job was done for the day. He was satisfied with his work and had nowhere to be. He decided he had earned some new clothes and started a vivacious stride with a smile on his face. Garcia truly loved roaming freely through the streets of Madrid. This was his city.

3.

David Harris and his wife, Rebecca, parked their BMW X3, gathered the luggage for Rebecca's trip and walked to the metro stop without saying a word to one another. David only bit at his fingernail tips, lost in his thoughts, as Rebecca looked in her compact mirror one last time. Rebecca's trips are usually only a few days. This time, however, her itinerary will last almost two weeks; the longest they have been apart in their five years of marriage.

The two met on a plane returning to D.C. from San Diego five and a half years prior. David was connecting in San Diego from Honolulu on return from an extended beach vacation with college friends, and Rebecca from a Pharmaceutical Industry conference. He fell in love with her eyes and their intoxicating green sparkle the moment they met. Her petite frame and angelic blonde hair were a comfortable familiarity for him. She was captivated by his soft heart and eager chivalrousness — his athletic build didn't hurt either. They spent the entire flight flirtatiously dancing in conversation and both knew before they landed that there was no possible way to live without each other any longer.

D.C. was Rebecca's hometown and David was from South Carolina. Rebecca was a successful general counsel for her employer, a pharmaceutical CRO. David had taken a sales job in the D.C. Metro area only a year prior that promised big commissions from government contracts, after several dead-end career choices.

David had previously been wallowing in his beachside, small hometown in South Carolina. It was no longer a place to live for a man in his position. He was a man without purpose. Clinging to his former girlfriend, he smothered her with his need for affirmation. Self-fulfilling his belief that she would leave him, she eventually did because of his lack of trust.

Waking up early in his empty one-bedroom apartment one morning — a year and a half prior to meeting Rebecca — he determined he would pack up his vehicle with his essentials despite the deafening apathy he was pinned down by. Something was pulling him out. It didn't matter where. Jogging his mind through the nearest regional cities, he rejected Atlanta, Charlotte and Jacksonville recognizing that he needed to get out of the south altogether. D.C., perhaps? He had only been there as a child to visit the Smithsonian Museums and the see the Declaration of Independence. Unclear as to what kept drawing his mind to D.C., he envisioned himself walking the streets, meeting new friends and going to hip restaurants. The Southern routine had worn his sensibilities thin. Nothing was left for him there in his hometown except for toxic friendships — and that was reason enough to move away from the small coastal, know-all-of-your-business milieu he'd grown up in. It was time for David to leave. The gossip and the prejudice, coupled with his increasing feeling of worthlessness, it was all becoming too much to handle in the face of all the adversity he had already dealt with in not being financially privileged, nor the pale complexion of his schoolmates.

I-95 North was a study in interminable frustration but David's mind was set and as he neared the capitol city only deciding on his destination seven hours earlier, he had already felt a new wind blowing his sails into town. It would be short-lived as most positive happenings tended to be in David's life. With all of his earthly belongings packed and no plan, David's naivety quickly reminded him of the reality of being alone in a new city. Finding a local real estate office was easy but finding an affordable apartment was not. After a week in a cheap motel, David settled in at a new loft apartment far outside the city and became a fast study of traffic patterns. He had his favorite restaurants picked out after the first month, though he couldn't afford them.

After three months, David's fresh sales job, selling furniture for relocating government employees, hadn't quite paid off and with the area housing market was booming he was almost evicted with nowhere to go. At the last possible moment, he finally closed a deal and paid off his back rent. He never had the opportunity to learn about making good financial choices from his parents. David barely made ends meet and things began to deteriorate in his new false utopia. He had no friends in the city and no family left. That's when he decided to join some college friends on a Hawaiian vacation — he became too desperate for companionship to miss it. The remaining cash he had left would fund his trip and pay for half of the rent when he returned. Though not as remarkable of a trip as he had hoped, going was the best decision he ever made.

His sun-kissed, thick, dark brown hair and caramel glow were re-touched by this recent Hawaiian adventure. Had he not met Rebecca on the flight back from that trip it was likely that he would have returned to South Carolina with his tail between his legs. He was thankful she met him after spending a week in the sun to touch him up, otherwise, she may have passed on his advance.

Upon arriving back home in D.C., the two dove head-first together. They spent most of their time at her loft apartment overlooking Georgetown's shopping district on Wisconsin Avenue. It was an easier drive to her office in DuPont Circle and she preferred the lively scene. David enjoyed that proxy life, pretending he belonged there and watching the rich spend their money. He knew he didn't belong. The gourmet pastries in the boulangerie a block away were enough to keep him happy — he wasn't overly interested in anything in the stores below. Rebecca, on the other hand, found great satisfaction in the procurement of the hautest of coutures. Rebecca and David visited his apartment only one time and never returned together. Her pleads for him to move in with her were met with a necessitative willingness despite his initial reservations.

David clung to Rebecca and the hope of building a new family with her. He was revitalized from the brink of near ruin. Rebecca, on the other hand, had a large family, was a socialite and had a successful career. Rebecca could see that David needed saving and relished the idea of bringing him home, much like she did with her stray dog, Bentley, that she brought home at age 11. She could fix David — she would clean him up and show off her accomplishment.

Their engagement was short and her friends were in shock that they fell in love so quickly. Rebecca had paid for the most extravagant ring by herself. Rebecca didn't want to have a large wedding despite her tendency toward the lavish when it came to her personal wardrobe. The small ceremony was quiet and David couldn't help the sense that Rebecca had intentionally not invited many of her socialite acquaintances. It had even only a few weeks before their marriage that David met Rebecca's parents for the first time. Her parents were less than pleased with the arrangement and vocalized their disdain for the pairing. It was within this dissonance, however, that they found unity. Rebecca was embarrassed by her father's blue collar upbringing. And, as David's were deceased, the pair were content to live out their lives free from in-laws, or at least with as little meddling as possible. Their passion for one another carried them through the trials and tribulations in the initial stages of their marriage and through all of the adversaries of their relationship. The need for one another bordered on co-dependency.

Rebecca enticed David to spend time abroad frequently — mostly on her family's dime despite her father's contempt for David. Rebecca's parents were intent on continuing their family tradition of summering abroad, regardless of whatever man Rebecca decided to bring along. Rebecca had, previously, brought a different man each time. Spain was the family's regular destination and overlooked her father's embarrassing, nouveau riche typical American caricature in order to maintain her appearance of a Jetsetter to her friends back home. David pretended to like the country on the first visit, but secretly, he deeply disliked it. His anxiety of travel and planes, not knowing his destination nor the people in it, predetermined his disdain for anywhere outside of his safety bubble, though Rebecca eventually convinced David to try living in Spain.

Conversations with Rebecca's father rarely went well and were focused on David's career. Rebecca's father knew David was not good enough for his daughter and would not be able to provide for her. He didn't care about David's skin color, only his lack of means. The obvious economic divide made Rebecca and David's relationship harder as time went on. Still, their love and bond were strong underneath the setting reality of their disparate perspectives on personal finances. They were both intentional, worked on their marriage and truly loved one another, but things had grown more complicated lately.

Nothing was ever as hard as when they had to say goodbye to one another, however. This time was especially hard. They had been out of rhythm lately and for the first time in their marriage, they had questioned being together. David had been missing his quotas at his sales job, again, distracted by doting over Rebecca. And, Rebecca was facing the prospect of multi-million-dollar deals about to fall through for her employer,

Parax Pharmaceuticals, if she didn't get her contracts signed before the end of the quarter. Though Rebecca didn't need the job and had her parents' money to fall back on, she excelled at her career and found purpose in it. Adding to her pressure, she had recently discovered a discrepancy in a fast-tracked, supposed miracle cancer drug that her company was representing – she had become consumed with detective work, knowing something wasn't right.

What little room was allowed for their relationship between their jobs was beginning to be squeezed out by the pressure put on them by their respective employers. It was a perfect storm for one of their rare blowouts. They had become shorter with each other in recent weeks and both were feeling increasingly distant from one another. A small crack was forming in their foundation. Rebecca was staying later at work, taking the odd visit to other offices overnight. David's suspicions of infidelity crept in like a whisper from a ghost.

Now, here at the Metro, there was nothing left but a short walk to the turnstile after a painfully quiet car ride. A brief embrace and a bittersweet, flaccid kiss, their palpable mutual anxiety was only muted by a lack of conversation as they let go of one another. David's eyes stared with heartache, hoping for some redemptive sign. Nothing. Rebecca was about to walk through the turnstile and took an eternity to turn around one last time. When she turned back to meet David's hopeful eyes, the blood rushed to her cheeks; the realization of her unending love for David returned in a flash and she ran into his welcoming arms. Everything, in that moment, for that instant at least, was resolved.

"I'm sorry I've been so distant David. I'll always love you and nothing will change that," Rebecca swore. David nodded and nuzzled into the nape of her neck, kissed her on the cheek and wished her bon voyage. David's heart sank – something told him this was the beginning of the end.

With a temporary bridge of reconciliation behind her, Rebecca walked through the Metro turnstile. As she entered the train, the British-accented "Doors Closing" announcement shifted her focus from her love. Riding to Reagan Airport while trying to ignore the horrible dank odor contained in the cabin, she slowly regained her focus on the purpose of her trip to Europe. She organized a meeting with her subordinate at Parax Pharmaceuticals — a pharmaceutical Contract Research Organization and her employer for the last seven years — to figure out just how her long-time overseas counterpart usurped her approval and had Rebecca's boss sign off on a contract that enabled a drug to make it to the next stage of development.

With her itinerary set for arrival at Madrid at 08:00 CET, she would have just enough time to check into her hotel to prepare before a lunch meeting with her colleague and her CEO, who had been working out of the Madrid office lately. Parax's travel department never asked when an employee would like to arrive and there was never any downtime on a work trip; maximizing employee output and profitability are always the first priority. The more contracts they win to test more drugs, the higher the profitability.

It had been an ongoing process for Rebecca to figure out how a recent study on a cancer treatment drug was green-lit by the FDA when, for the past several years, she herself saw the mid-study interim analyses, all of which fell short of the FDA mandated primary endpoints that were supposed to clearly indicate medical improvement.

There was no way that drug should have made it as far as it did. Even with the assumption that the Business Development salespeople would be fast-tracking every angle they could so they could sit back and collect their commissions as they always did, it made no sense to Rebecca. Being the persistent, and some would call anal-retentive, worker that she was, she was dead set on both absolving herself and fully unraveling how

RXG1 made it this far.

Rebecca reserved her most infinitely granular scrutiny for the RXG1 contract. Her intuition led her to feel that she had to pay special attention to this one. She had been warned by her superior the day prior not to dig too deep and pleaded with her to take some time off, and that she was exhibiting signs of being burned out. The "Miracle Cancer Drug" from the Valencian Bioscience contract had been consuming her lately, drastically affecting her normal workload capacity. It had been a struggle for her lately to maintain her daily life, marriage, friendships and hobbies, let alone her day-to-day work responsibilities when she knew something was wrong.

As the head of her legal department, her neck was always on the line to get contracts approved from a fiscal standpoint from the company, however, the FDA would be quick to attack her if there were any inconsistencies whatsoever. She walked a fine line between the customers, the company and the FDA, and her days were taut with friction from all sides wanting every sliver of time from her. As a woman of conviction, she couldn't rest until she figured out how this drug, she recommended to be prevented from phase 2 testing, progressed through the ranks under her nose.

RXG1, the drug in question, was a venture by Valencian Bioscience, a Spanish based company and leader of the industry. They were a stock investor's dream and one of the most difficult-to-work-with companies Rebecca had the displeasure of collaborating with. Known for their outlandish PR claims during the production of new drugs that would cure everything from male baldness to AIDS, no doubt in order to stimulate their shareholders, they spared no expense in theatrics. Since Valencian was a client, she had to always bow to their demands, but whenever she scrupulously reviewed their contracts and data, there was always a shortfall and a diversion clearly aimed at getting their drugs to the final statistical analysis phase. The final statistical analysis phase – a crucial final step in getting a packet submitted – in RXG1's case, was of particular importance since its studies were to be conducted in both the U.S. and Spain and submitted to the Spanish Ministry of Health and the FDA for approval. However, given the right circumstances and willing hands, this phase could be easily tampered with. Falsifying data to win a regulatory agencies' approval, though far-fetched in Rebecca's mind, could have, technically, been achieved. Only a biostatistician in the upper echelons of a Contract Research Organization, typically a CEO, could have altered or tampered with these packets.

With the Valencian Bioscience contract in question, their meteoric rise in the stock market in the last quarter and their phantom-like approval in the final stages, Rebecca saw a red flag. She sensed something was afoul. No "Miracle Drug" for cancer, or any high-profile drug for that matter, should have made it through the Phase 1 trials that quickly, let alone all the way through Phase 3. Phase 1 consists of healthy volunteers and the results were not promising with dozens of reported side-effects, so it was unsettling to Rebecca to know it had been fast-tracked through Phase 2, while Phase 3 and was ready to hit the market. Her suspicions that something wasn't right, began in the fall earlier that year. With pressure from her superiors to process Valencian Bioscience's contracts faster than the others, which is not necessarily uncommon for high-profile, high-profit products such as theirs, she couldn't help but come to affirm the logical assumption that money is always the driving force behind any of these drugs. Whether it was an uncommon affliction or a worldwide epidemic, the race to a cure was neither fueled by the need to better humanity, nor a need to save lives; it was to meet shareholders' expectations and fill the pockets of those in power. While it may take the sales of an erectile dysfunction pill to fund the research needed to find a cure for the big ones like cancer, it never fully sat well with Rebecca.

Her developing jaded outlook on her industry was further bemoaned when several new cosmetic enhancement drugs were picked up in lieu of a major HIV study that could have saved people. But HIV was dead to the shareholders. People are smarter these days, or at least more informed; they use protection. And if they're not smart enough, they sure as hell can't pay for an expensive prescription. That's how her boss framed it to her, at least. The study's demise and subsequent, and more profitable, replacement was only one of the many examples of Rebecca's growing resentment.

The whole reason she got into the pharmaceutical industry in the first place, was to feel like she was making a difference in the world. Her contribution, though small, in taking her first job with the company as a contract analyst, would mean something; she would have stood for bettering the world's health as she worked her way through nights, weekends and lunch breaks. She was a firm believer in "better living through science," and though the corporate life bogged her lofty ideals down as she drudgingly earned her way to the top of the legal department, she hoped that she would have a say-so once she made it there. It came in the form of day-to-day decisions; decisions to place more effort on getting contracts approved for drugs that mattered to the real world, for people with real health issues, not whatever new nonsensical, fabricated ailment that seemingly would materialize in new variations every month. She called them the "flavor-of-the-month diseases", like Restless Leg Syndrome. Sure, the remote possibility of one of these flavors of the month might bring some comfort and vitality to a couple of lives, but not anything that stretching, exercising and eating healthily wouldn't do for them in the first place.

Then, there was Ana Esperanza. She was Rebecca's nemesis at Valencian Bioscience, the company Project Manager and her company's client. Intolerably arrogant and invariably wrong about their arguments over inconsequential data findings, Ana, the ever-micro-manager, was extremely pushy when it came to Rebecca processing their documents expeditiously.

Rebecca never trusted Ana's word and had a feeling that she and Richard had been in contact ... and just maybe ... they had to have colluded in some fashion, Rebecca resolved.

Rebecca was dreading their upcoming meeting at Parax's Madrid office on this trip. She was insufferable. Rebecca knew that these discrepancies would bury Ana this time though. Rebecca had previously believed her CEO, Richard Blackwell, had her back, even encouraging the face-to-face meeting at the Madrid office to sort it out, despite asking her to take time off just weeks prior. Now she wasn't so sure. He always talked out of both sides of his mouth and she saw right through him. But why had Richard signed off on this contract without Rebecca at least getting a once over in the first place? She was puzzled by the sudden change in tone from Richard lately; he had been replacing his typical shrugging off of Rebecca's needling requests to go by-the-book with a more proactive intercession. His change of heart was disconcerting. First, he wanted her to take a break from this contract, now he's facilitating a meeting for her to resolve it with Valencian directly. It nagged at her. She couldn't leave this thought alone.

The Metro ride was long but it afforded her the opportunity to collate her shuffled thoughts. She was focused, driven and always set on giving work her all. She never left a stone unturned and reviewed every pathway. Trudging through the hordes of passengers at her airport stop, she remembered why she hated riding the Metro and wished David had just driven her over — he would have been sitting in traffic for hours after her drop-off and didn't want to curse him with that burden. Besides, left to his own devices, it probably would have set David off into road-rage and he might have hurt someone. She could sense that tension was boiling beneath his exterior facade and had been intentionally avoiding stirring him up lately. He hadn't been himself and she knew he never properly dealt with the loss of his parents. It was his job that was wearing him down too — he was drowning while she was thriving. She knew he was becoming jealous of her success but he chose to ignore it and bottle it up along with the rest of his bad luck.

Rebecca loved to fly and loved the thrill of international travel regardless of how many times she had done it. It helped her to feel accomplished, purposeful, as her old sorority sisters languished in suburbia with babies on their hips. With that thought, she happily waited in the security checkpoints and smiled as she handed the gate agent her ticket when they called for first class passengers to board. She only flew first class.

Sitting down in her oversized chair in the last row of first class, Rebecca's eyes met an elderly Spanish woman as she made her way past Rebecca on her way to economy class directly behind where Rebecca was sitting. The elderly woman's eyes pierced through Rebecca, giving Rebecca a chillingly odd, vulnerable sensation. It was as if this woman knew exactly who Rebecca was and everything she had ever done. She could feel her eyes piercing the back of her head for several minutes.

Despite this uneasy awkwardness, Rebecca's plight with her company and her upcoming meeting trumped this peculiar, gypsy-like woman's spell. Something didn't quite feel right about the flight, this strange woman and, more importantly, this meeting. It was as if the forces of the universe were propelling her to some unknown inevitability all of a sudden. Even though Parax sent employees around the World without discretion, why were they really sending her to Madrid to throw her findings in Ana's face? And why was Richard so accommodating with this? The revelatory, sinking feeling that Richard had orchestrated this, at least in-part, filled Rebecca with dread.

4.

Madrid Barajas International Airport, 17 June 6:50 a.m. CET

Those red eye flights across the Atlantic leave most travelers bleary-eyed. Not Rebecca. Her focus was now squarely upon Richard after a long flight of scanning documents and piecing the puzzle together in her mind. She was intent, resolute. Richard was at the center of it all. That much she knew.

The landing gear jolting against the runway shook Rebecca, but it didn't waiver her thoughts for a second. The only distraction was that of the buzzing of her phone in her pocket as she collected the stack of study results she had been up all night combing through. She had forgotten to turn it off during takeoff. It was Richard. His name popping up on screen startled her; she

contemplated not answering but picked up after three rings.

"Here we go," she said to herself as she lifted the phone to her ear.

"Hi Richard ... no, I just landed," her heart racing, she responded to his request, "No that's fine, I'll meet you in front of baggage claim in 30 minutes, I still have to go through customs."

He was already on his way to pick her up from the airport himself. Parax usually sent a driver but this time it was Richard. *'That can't be good,'* she thought to herself as she hung up. Her original plan was to check into the hotel and get settled first. She decided, however, that now was good as a time as any – she'd rip the Band-Aid off. She would let Richard know that she knew he was involved. She trembled with anxiety as she stood up and waited to disembark.

"¿Oye, senora, podrías ayudarme con mi equipaje?" the little old Spanish lady requested, ribbing Rebecca with her bony elbow out of her frazzled trance.

'This old witch wants help with her luggage after she cast her spell on me?' Rebecca thought in her sharp, wry wit.

She was an inconvenient roadblock and it frustrated Rebecca, yet she politely obliged as it was her nature to do so. Rebecca pulled the vintage suitcase down from the overhead bin and set it down. The line moved. Only Rebecca and the old lady were left at the front of the line, with the rest of the passengers waiting behind them, impatiently shuffling and muttering under their breath. Rebecca turned to hurry on her way – a firm skeletal grip on her arm prevented her.

She turned back towards the old lady who stared into her eyes again, "Donde quiera que vayas ... ey ... where you are going

... ey ... you will be okay."

Confused, Rebecca cocked her head quizzically in response.

"The cross ... the cross I see around your neck ..." pointing to Rebecca's cross necklace that her deceased grandmother gave her during her childhood that she always wore.

"... He will be waiting for you, siempre ... always."

Rebecca, now even more confused, could only utter a one-word reply, "Gracias," as she briskly walked, almost running, down the aisle to exit the plane and escape the clutches of the oracle.

The school-bus yellow arches adorning the modern airport reminded her of where she was. She had loved Spain. After many travels there, it was her favorite country and her favorite language. The lisp of the theta pronunciation in their dialect was an endearing quality to her. And though customs took more than 30 minutes to get through, the Guardia Civil agent's accent was enough to do the trick for Rebecca. She cracked a smile for him and gave a perfectly pronounced "Grathias" back for him.

The luggage always took for what seemed to be an eternity to arrive at baggage claim at Madrid-Barajas. Today, the wait was excruciating. Rebecca – left to the purgatory of her mind for even longer – pondered what she would say to Richard, attempting to shake off the old lady's haunting encounter. Richard would never admit to being involved in such malfeasance – his pseudo-Southern charm would snake around any obstacle. He could sell anything and make you feel good about yourself for believing in him. Rebecca always knew it was all a facade with Richard, but she never thought he would be engaged in corruption. Rebecca was talented at suffering fools gladly, but occasionally her naiveté got the best of her. She would freely lend trust and a gentle warmness, but if she was burned, she went after the violator with an unrelenting vengeance. She was the embodiment of the phrase, 'Hell hath no fury like the woman scorned' when provoked. She shared this trait with her husband David, and it was a strong commonality that bonded them.

Rebecca became infuriated with Richard – if he truly had a hand in fast-tracking this cancer drug, whether it was tampering with CRAs' field reports or downright lying in their reports to the FDA, then everything she knew about him was a truly a lie. He didn't care about the patients or making the World a better place; he only cared about lining his pockets like the rest of them. She felt embarrassed for having given him the benefit of the doubt, for laughing at the jokes he told, sitting on the edge of her desk and asking her how her personal life was at the end of a long day. "That son-of-a-b ..." she began to think to herself, as a silver-haired Spanish man abruptly placed his hand on her arm, "Eh, Ms. Rebecca?"

"Yes?" she replied, startled.

"Eh, señora, the Mr. Richard Blackwell, he ... he is waiting in the car outside for you. I am Javier Guaita. I will escort you to him. Por favor, deja que te ayude ... please, let me help you with your bags," the man emphatically replied in his broken, child-like English. Accosted for a second time by a complete stranger in under an hour, Rebecca pondered her own fate for the first time.

With the feeling of being ambushed setting in, Rebecca, having no time to go to the hotel and reset after a long flight, and, having reluctantly agreed to have Richard pick her up, and yet still, having a strange Spaniard in a Valencian Bioscience polo shirt essentially grab and escort her to the car, was pissed.

Rebecca walked into the sunlight of the Madrid morning in front of the airport with this man as she watched Richard, the ever-handsome silver fox, step out of the back seat of the black Mercedes S Class parked at the curb and adjust his Prada blazer.

"Rebecca my dear, I'm so glad to see you. Did you get to

sleep on the plane? Those flights can be murder," he said to Rebecca said his charming, educated, southern accent.

"No, no I didn't. Listen, Richard, I know there's a lot on the docket today, but we need to talk ... in private, Richard," Rebecca curtly replied, motioning with her eyes to imply Javier Guaita.

"Oh that's just Javier, he barely speaks English. Valencian Bioscience sent him to drive me around while I'm here. He's the head of their security team. He's been quite helpful, actually. Don't worry about him; let's talk. You're staying at the Petit Palace Savoy Alfonso XII, right? We'll take you there," Richard said gesturing to Javier to get Rebecca's bags and put them in the trunk.

The smell of the diesel fuel wafting through the air of the airport road was giving Rebecca a headache. She was tired now. She obliged Richard and got into the back seat of the Mercedes. Javier made a call from his cell phone as he loaded her bag and walked to the front of the car. The conversation – muffled and in Spanish – distracted Rebecca, she felt unnerved by some of the words she picked up. She was fluent in Spanish, but his dialect and slang were hard to understand, perhaps it was Catalán.

"Rebecca," Richard said, drawing her attention out of listening in, "You wanted to tell me something?"

"Richard ... what is going on with the Valencian Bioscience cancer study?" Rebecca blurted out without any restraint.

Richard shuffled to a more assertive upright position in his seat; Javier's eyes glanced back at them from the rearview mirror as he drove away from the airport terminal.

She continued, "There's no reason why this study has progressed as quickly as it has without people ... or someone ... altering the data. How is it already under priority review? I know you have to be aware of how this happened And why didn't you tell me ... everything?"

"Rebecca, dear, you shouldn't be so troubled. Everything is perfectly fine, I'm meeting with the Valencian Bioscience people this afternoon and I will get everything cleared up. Let's get you to your hotel so you can relax and recoup from the flight. You trust me, don't you?" Rebecca, mildly disarmed by his charm, took a deep breath and nodded as exhaustion set in.

The ride into the Madrid city center seemed shorter than normal. Javier interjected over his shoulder towards Richard in the backseat, as they made their way through the arches of Puerta de Alcalá and onto Gran Vía. Javier should have made a left onto Paseo de Prado, Rebecca mentally noted, and he instead continued into the heart of the city. "Señor, the traffic, es desmasiado ... we will be here for hours and we won't make the meeting."

Richard obliged, "That's okay, Javier."

"Rebecca, you won't mind if we drop you off at this square do you? Your hotel is just a couple of blocks away ... it's a very short walk. Stop and grab a café con leche, there's a great little spot in there. You have any Euros? Here's €100."

Rebecca, feeling lambasted by Richard's preparedness, declined the money. "Yes, okay, that's fine. I don't need your money. I could use the walk anyway, but I just want you to know ... this isn't settled. I need to know why this cancer drug has been fast-tracked." She continued defiantly just before closing her door as she exited, "... and I know you're involved."

Richard leered at her through the tinted window without responding.

"Pop it!" Rebecca shouted at Javier from the rear of the car. The dry-cleaned Guardia Civil uniform, still in its plastic, in the trunk seemed peculiar to her but her anger demanded her attention more.

She pulled the bag from the car and looked around. Her agenda, now shelved by Richard's charisma, would have to wait until the evening.

The rich smells of Spain – the panaderías, perfumerias and the dry, hot air – gave her a fleeting sense of comfort, if only for a moment. It was a much longer walk than Richard let on. She was back in Spain, a country she loved and hadn't been to since the last trip two years ago with David. They fought a lot during that trip. Yet somehow they would effortlessly repair their bond through humor and would easily laugh at things together, especially at the street performers wearing the knock-off superheroes' and children's characters' costumes. And here was Elmo to greet her in the square where she last saw him, still overweight, not the right color red and matted, dirty fuzz. She smirked and rolled her luggage across the cobblestones, unaware of the predatory eyes following her every move.

5.
Georgetown, Washington, D.C., USA, 18 June 3:37 a.m. EST

David's cell phone buzzed on his nightstand. Hungover from the night's prior self-loathing, his brains swelled to throb his skull to the rhythm of the caller. He knew it would be Rebecca calling to check back in after their brief conversation after her flight. He had been worried and drank to stay up to hear her initial call upon arrival around 2 a.m., his time. He watched movies alone and sipped Jim Beam, neat, until he would hear her voice. He knew those journeys across the ocean only to go straight into work aren't for the faint of heart, and that Rebecca would be okay. As he wiped the slumber from his eyes, he felt relieved to know that she had remembered to call later in her day. Sometimes she forgot. She was perpetually distracted with work but he always waited for her. The same as he did as a boy waiting for his parents to return — they never did.

The turn-of-the-century wood floor boards moaned with age underneath David's feet as he sat up from the bed. It was always cold in the bedroom in their modest — by Rebecca's family's standards — colonial row house, even in the summer. The home was handed down to them on their wedding by Rebecca's grandmother. Though a highly sought after locale, David had a disdain for the property. He felt trapped by it and by Rebecca's encroaching and overbearing family. Being alone in it made him feel more isolated than he had when he was still single. He didn't choose it. And every item in the home was ushered in by Rebecca's family and friends. His signature wasn't found in the home, nor on the deed.

The number wasn't Rebecca's, but began with Spain's +34 country code. Calling from her hotel room probably, he thought to himself.

"Hello?" he answered. There was a long pause from the caller.

"Eh, Señor, Harris?" the voice of the female, Spanish caller asked.

"Uh ... yes, who is this?" he apprehensively responded. His heart began racing.

"Eh, Señor, Harris, my name is Camila Abaroa, I am the Deputy Inspector for the Minsterio del Interior ... eh la Policia for Madrid, España. I'm sorry, but I have some troubling news for you. Por favor, please, sit down if you are not already. To confirm, you are Señor David Harris ... marido ... eh, husband to a one Rebecca Harris, no?"

David's head spinning with questions, "Yea ... yes, ahem, yes. What is this about?"

The woman's voice, crackled, "Señor Harris, your wife, she ... we found her body this morning in the Petit Palace Savoy Alfonso XII hotel ... aqui en Madrid. I am very sorry to be the one to tell you this señor. She is ... deceased, Señor Harris."

David thought he was dreaming for a moment, closing his eyes, he saw Rebecca's face. His heart sank deep into the darkness.

"Señor Harris, are you there?"

He wasn't dreaming. It took him several moments to find his voice. He was in disbelief.

"That's preposterous, Inspector. She ... she ... I just talked to her last night ... I ... don't understand ... what?"

His thoughts drifted to Rebecca in her wedding dress,

remembering their great love when they first met, her beautiful and sweet face, her radiating smile. He began sobbing uncontrollably. He wished he had told her he loved her more. That he was sorry for all of the hurtful things he said to her over the years. Nothing could take it all back. David knew that the police inspector was telling the truth. In that moment, he knew that her soul had gone from the earth. Several minutes passed as David zoned out into an out-of-body-like state.

"Señor Harris, are you still there?" the inspector asked after gracing him a few more moments to collect himself.

"What ... what happened to her?" David asked as his voice quivered.

"Eh, Señor Harris ... this is potentially upsetting; we found her hanged ... we are filing the report as ... em ... suicidio ... eh ... suicide."

'How could she?' David thought to himself.

David changed his tone to indignant, "Forgive me ... you mean to tell me that my wife committed suicide? That wouldn't ... she wouldn't ... you must have your facts wrong. Are you sure? I ... don't under... she ... she killed herself?"

The inspector, reserved her suspicions about the crude nature of the suicide, "We will be reviewing the security footage, but Señor Harris we will need you to come to España to identify the ..." She paused, not wanting to be callous, empathizing with David, "... to, eh ... we need you to come, are you available to come right away? The U.S. Bureau of Consular Affairs should also be contacting you ... have you heard from them?"

The state of shock not settling in, David leaned on his best social skill to maintain his composure, "Abaroa. Tell me, Ms. Abaroa. Where are you from? Your last name ... what does it mean?" David asked.

"I don't understand … eh, me llamo … ah, my surname … my people are from the Basque country, it means refugio … eh … refuge." Camila obliged kindly. The out-of-context questioning allowed David a sense of calm for a moment; long enough to regain a grip on reality.

"I always like to know where people come from — what their names mean — it helps me to understand them a little better."

David continued, "Inspector, I am having trouble … I don't … I can't believe she would do this to me. How could she do that?" David retuned to sobbing.

"Take your time."

"I … I'm sorry, Inspector. To answer your question, yes, I will look online for a flight right away and try to get there as soon as possible."

Nothing felt real. Nothing made sense. David felt the walls of the row home closing in on him. Rebecca would not have done this. There's no way, he thought. Then, he remembered their last kiss — something didn't feel right, as if she wasn't there. Maybe she was unhappy. Depressed people can sometimes hide it — David certainly knew how.

David's anxiety tremors shook him more violently than they ever had before. He did not want to get on a plane and fly across the ocean. He did not want to interact with strangers and pretend like everything was okay. He did not want to see his wife's corpse, lying lifeless on a cold steel table.

"Email me your itinerary when you complete your, eh … bookings. Write down my email."

David scrambled for a pen, Camila's voice was somehow becoming familiar, pleasant even.

David took Camila's contact information and address, said goodbye and hung up the phone. His eyes wandered listlessly around the room. The house was silent, cold. The walls retracted.

Their home, beautiful and dilapidated, a talented and loving wife and yet, David couldn't break out of the sadness and frustration he had felt every day — even before today. He knew he should have been a happier person but his life felt without purpose. The moments of joy were always when he was with Rebecca, and regardless of their less-than-perfect marriage, she still made him smile. Still, the anxiety and depression rolled like a tidal wave, exponentially growing larger and causing more destruction in his life as time went on. Maybe he drove her to do this to herself, he thought.

Rebecca was his crown and his only positive accomplishment. He married up, out of a singular and crashing existence. He had no true home and his family were all dead. He never confronted the death of his mother and father as a child and that set up a basecamp of disappointing life decisions from there on out. Depression gripped his throat.

Despite their occasional foolish argument over marital roles and David's insecurities, she was the best thing David had going. She also emasculated him. Overshadowed by her personal and professional success, David's limitations were only amplified. Unable to channel his frustration, the only solution was to shut down and hide himself inside the echo chamber of his own mind. She helped him push his anger deeper below the surface. She didn't have time anymore to deal with it. The newness was wearing off, just like it did with her dog, Bentley.

David had grown to be a quiet man in recent years. He was a do-nothing, lost in his own mind. This sudden loss of Rebecca was about to freeze him to a solid state. The humiliation of life's disappointments had finally worn him down, as it tends to do to men in their 30s. Relegated to mediocrity in his own personal achievements and overshadowed by his overachieving and and intelligent wife's accomplishments, David withdrew. He banished himself to obscurity rather than have his shortcomings exposed. Anxiety consumed him all the time now, especially around his newly acquired city friends. David grew suspicious of these people for no apparent reason, as if they were conspiring against him and were bent on seeing him fail at every turn. He knew they laughed at him behind his back. He could never get it quite right; a failed business idea here, a wrong path there and all he had to show for all of this toiling to find meaning and purpose was a few white hairs that had begun to sprout in his dark brown waves in the last several months.

Anger began to manifest itself in the most inane circumstances; a door not closing properly; dishes left in the sink overnight; someone not using their blinker. It had always been lurking under the surface and he never properly dealt with the loss of his family. David was capable of a terrifying rage. Quietly, it waited for just the right time to surface.

David sat dumbfounded that his wife was dead. She had killed herself. Hanged. She took a rope and hung herself. It was his fault. David replayed it over and over for hours as the pains in his stomach churned. His heart ached. Rebecca was gone. He couldn't decide if he should be mad at her or if he should start crying. His body chose for him. The bidding of rage.

David's paranoia and frustration were about to strike a final, lethal blow to his marriage with Rebecca. The silence of his inaction began to wear Rebecca thin. He refused to see a counselor, to be ambitious or excited about anything, to leave his lonely mind. That is, until this day. This day, David's anxiety, depression and paranoia were now full term, grown as a hideous creature inside of him. This day, David's quiet demon that had been slightly scratching at the surface, began the birthing pangs within him. The chrysalis of decorum cracked and flaked away as its wings unfurled in preparation to spread wide. Rage was born and ready to explode from his viscera.

He began just knocking a few things over. A picture of

45

them together, a piece of pottery they bought together in Spain, and soon, larger items followed.

After several hours, broken doors, windows and various ceramic accoutrements, and bloodied fists, David satiated the rage enough to fall to the floor in exhaustion. David rationalized that someone must've called the police with all of the incalculable destruction he had just caused to the poor old house. Sirens never sounded, police never came. David's sheer fatigue finally gave way to uncontrollable tears.

It was almost dusk by the time David came back to life. He scraped his own body up from the floor. Floating around the house in disbelief and out-of-body, he surveyed the damage and made his way to the master bedroom.

David had a thought as he sat down on the bed, *'I did this to her. I drove her to this. I'm worthless. How ... how could she do it? She didn't deserve to die — I do.'*

He dove further into the void.

David got up and looked for instruments to cut into his flesh. Scattering items in drawers, searching, anything. The kitchen. Suicidal thoughts occasionally visited David but now they had moved in. David grabbed his chef's knife that he had used to chop onions for soup the day prior and plunged it towards his stomach, stopping at the last possible second. He wanted to die but became too afraid to do it to himself. His fear had no face, no description — it was simply the fear of the unknown. David dropped the knife and it clattered loudly on the floor. He didn't even have the fortitude to do himself in — he felt pathetic. His own depression prevented him from the happy marriage he wanted so desperately; it also prevented him from taking his own life. His depression held him in an inescapable prison.

Suddenly, Rebecca appeared to him. Her vision consumed his mind and reminded him that she was lovely and smart and everything he wasn't.

David's mind raced, 'Maybe … maybe she … maybe she *didn't* do this. Maybe…'

David searched for his laptop, which he hoped he didn't smash in his blind rage. David suddenly and unexpectedly had a will to live, a direction. Though only moments earlier he was gripped by depression like a hand around his throat, the feeling was temporarily replaced with a clarifying purpose. He felt like a different person altogether. Reaching under the bed, his hand found that the laptop was still intact. He opened it and booked his ticket to Madrid. It was the same red-eye flight schedule that Rebecca had been on.

With only a few hours before the flight to Madrid-Barajas Airport departed, David rushed around the house, grabbed his passport, a few items of clothing and threw them into a bag. He locked the door behind him and made his way to the Metro to get to Reagan Airport. As the metro doors closed behind him, the automated announcement in an out-of-place British accent, "Doors Closing" reminded David of how Rebecca always thought that the announcement sounded like "George Clooney". He wanted to smile but he forced himself not to.

The stops in between gave David time, just as they had with Rebecca, to think and remember one of the last conversations he had with her. Something about Valencian Bioscience, and rushing a cancer drug to market, he thought. He remembered that she seemed alarmed, though David shrugged it off at the time, attributing it to her typical tenacity for perfection. He had never worked in the pharmaceutical field, but over the years of listening to Rebecca, he had gleaned a few pertinent details. He knew what the phases in clinical trials were, he knew that the FDA had stringent laws; however, they could sometimes be lax depending on the drug, the client and the current administration. He knew that nothing got past Rebecca, and he knew that her boss, Richard Blackwell was a weasel. David saw right through Richard's feigned attempts at southern charm. David saw him slink off with an administrative assistant at a company Christmas party one year and had, ever since, picked up on other strange behaviors at their occasional encounters. He knew Richard had a thing for Rebecca. David tried to convince Rebecca she should change companies and get out from working for Richard. He had thought that she couldn't see through Richard's sleeze. It pissed him off when she defended Richard and was the source of frequent fights.

It had occurred to David that there was a conversation she had with Ana Esperanza – she hated Ana – and something about her client, Valencian Bioscience, fast-tracking this cancer drug and that somehow Ana falsified some paperwork. Rebecca had been complaining about Ana after work for weeks now.

"That's right! Rebecca was going to *bust* her ass on this trip!" David said aloud as the revelation came to fruition in his mind. The other passengers on the Metro ignored the disheveled man with blood on his knuckles talking to himself. They were used to the crazies. David didn't care anyway. He found a thread. And he was going to pull until it was all unraveled. The pointlessness and despair David had been feeling that had sharply disappeared earlier were not even a memory anymore. He needed to find out why she killed herself— and if.

After making his way through the airport, the ticket counter and security, David sat down at a quiet gate – a rarity for Reagan National – to calm his wildly racing mind down. Ana Esperanza kept popping into his mind like a broken record, repeating her name to himself, almost involuntarily. He knew she was the common thread. He thought of Spain. He fumed so much in his chair that he began to sweat. David sat irritated thinking about being back there until group 8 was called to board.

As his flight boarded, David began drifting into thoughts of Rebecca. David wished he could talk to his wife just one more time. The weight of her loss paralyzed him in his window seat for the duration of the flight. The hurt ached his bones. He drifted in and out of a dream-like state, haunted by his own shortcomings as a husband, dreaming of his wife and all the things he wished he hadn't done and hadn't said. He pictured her – the longing was unbearable. He sat miserably, knees smashed by economy class seats. His lower back ached from the unnatural shape his 6'3 body made to accommodate the inhumane, gargoyle-overlooking-a-cathedral-like formation. The flight was a blur of emotions and anxiety and as his plane touched down in Madrid, his resolve crystalized in the same way Rebecca's did upon arrival.

With only his carry-on, David breezed through those stupid yellow arches. He hated yellow. Of course the Spanish would paint their airport yellow. '*Morons*,' David thought.

The customs line was a mile long and David had to piss the entire time. David registered, standing there, that he hated everything about the country and the people. David reveled in being the walking stereotype of a rude American, as he said "thanks" in defiant English to the Spanish agent, finally passing through. Spain was always a sore subject between David and Rebecca. They had traveled there on holiday a couple of times and David liked Spain okay at first, but then the more accurate memory came into clarity — that of Rebecca pushing David to travel there. Her attempts to persuade him to move there were fruitless. David's memories only served his contempt for the country. Their dependence on socialistic traditions passed down from earlier generations — that sense of entitlement when walking down a street, standing in a line waiting for a coffee or a baguette. The pushing — they were pushy. The fallacy of monarchy blended with a long history of socialism and now democracy and capitalism was confusing, and it was no wonder the result was a confused country and people. The euro-to-dollar conversion; the inability to afford anything luxurious; the graffiti; the grime; the stupid Spaniards and their

emphatic gesturing over inane details, like the cultural significance of mariscos from Galicia. All of it ruined Spain. And of
course, there was the heat. It was too much for him — the lack of
widespread air-conditioning didn't help.

David had made up his mind by now; essentially, Spain
was responsible for the degradation of his marriage and now,
the death of his wife.

David walked out of the airport and onto the curbside
taxi pick-up waiting area in nearly the same spot that his deceased wife stood in only days prior. Without warning, tears
streamed down his face as he came to this realization – he was
physically and emotionally exhausted. A cab pulled up and he
wiped his face. David asked the driver to take him to the Municipal Police station in the feeblest of attempts at Spanish. He'd
been nearly conversational at one point. Most of it, intentionally forgotten. David had been numb up until this point – the
day had already heated up and David was sweating. He got into
the well air-conditioned cab. Thank God, he thought.

The cab driver didn't say a single word to David as he
weaved through the traffic on Paseo de Prado. David wondered
if Rebecca had taken this same route the day before. The driver
had picked up on the duress clearly worn on David's face and
disheveled demeanor and decided to cut back his normal small
talk with passengers. Living up to David's perceived stereotype
as opportunists, the Spaniard decided to take this sad sack,
dumb American the long way. David knew the driver was taking
him on a roundabout way to the police station – he didn't care.
It gave him time to collect himself before meeting with the
Deputy Inspector, Abaroa.

Passing the Parque Retiro, David recognized a familiar
scene and cracked the window to a familiar combination of
scents: the trees, diesel exhaust, designer cologne and churro
vendors. He remembered that the last time he was in Spain with
Rebecca, they had strolled through the park, laid on a blanket,

drank some cheap red wine and kissed. The warm memory made him crack a smile. There were no cares in those days. Strolling from their rented flat to a nearby plaza, they did a little window shopping and the odd escaping of the heat by casually slipping into clothing stores he couldn't afford to cool off in the only free air conditioning. A café mid-morning, some patatas bravas, a cana and sangria by 11, and one of the 10€ menu del dias at a dive bar – always inevitably featuring squid ink in some form or another in one of the plates. All in time for a nap in the park by 1.

They spent the bulk of their personal savings coming to Spain on their last extended trip, though Rebecca's trust fund remained untouched. It was meant to be a reboot in their relationship. They sold most of their personal belongings, along with David's car and saved up for a year for this. For David, it was a risk, but he hated his job at the time and knew that they needed to break away from Rebecca's doting and overbearing family. The final step was quitting their jobs – only, Rebecca didn't actually quit. She had continued her work for Parax remotely, causing an additional rift between them. Rebecca subversively pushed the idea of living in Spain full-time even more passive-aggressively during that trip. At that time, Parax's operations were focusing in on RXG1 and living in Spain was as viable as an option as ever. Her dream come true.

There David was, in Spain, jobless, as his wife continued her corporate climbing. David didn't last long as the accessory to Rebecca. He implored and eventually convinced her after only six weeks in the country, to move back home so he could find work.

Reticently, Rebecca conceded and at her behest, convinced her father to utilize his network to land David another sales job upon their return to D.C. Her father always took care of everything for her – they never could've have afforded their Georgetown digs on Rebecca's salary, let alone David's.

David's smile faded as he recollected the rest of the memory. Spain was no longer fun.

The police station stood ominous and regal, with armed officers holding MP4s guarding the front entrance. As the cab driver pulled up, David's stomach turned to knots with anxiety. David paid the driver the inflated rate, got out of the cab, looked up at the building and into the sky as the morbid thought of his wife's corpse laying lifeless crept in. He shivered in the heat of the day and started chewing on his nails incessantly.

Awaiting the appointment with the American widower, Inspector Camila Abaroa sat at her desk looking at pictures on her ex-husband's social media profiles when she was called to the receptionist's desk up front. She didn't hear the call and continued scrolling the pages. She rarely indulged in such diminutive distractions but she couldn't help this one. The picture of the bikini-clad, young bimbo on her ex-husband's arm incensed her – it was always Camila's idea to sail around Ibiza. She had helped put a down payment on the vessel with Hector, and now here he was living her dream with someone else. With a much younger woman at his side in the picture, she felt a sense of relief knowing she didn't have to deal with him anymore, but also a sense of remorse for the unwitting girl. Camila wanted to sail around Ibiza since she was a young girl herself but never had the means. That's when Hector came along and bulldozed himself into her life. They were always strapped for cash as government employees during their brief relationship. All of a sudden, here is Hector, a terminated cop and divorcee, boasting about sailing around the Mediterranean on the sailboat that they could barely afford before. Money was their most disputed argument when they were married for those four years. She had married too young, regrettably, to a fellow police officer. Their short marriage was marred with heated arguments and her suspicions of infidelity were confirmed in short order. Hector was incorrigible. It's what first attracted her to him — he was relentless when she joined the force. She was depressed, lonely and away from home. Hector came at a time when she needed him to.

Hector's behavior became erratic when pressed about his finances towards the end. He had a sudden change in wardrobe and began making ancillary purchases with money that Camila never saw. That's what drove them to separate. When the department began their internal investigation into Hector and his misdeeds began, Camila knew it was time to end it completely. His tenure as an officer ended abruptly when he was formally accused of extorting bribes from local criminals. His marriage followed suit immediately thereafter. Spaniards rarely divorce regardless of infidelities but Camila was not one to waste time and heeded her instinct that she priorly neglected concerning Hector — he was no good. But still, where or from whom was he getting the money?

Camila's eyes lifted and met David Harris' as the light coming in from the window obscured his figure and he came into focus. His tall, well-framed body, light brown skin, dark hair and blue eyes caught Camila off guard. He had been directed to her desk when she failed to answer the receptionist's call. He didn't need to introduce himself; she knew immediately by his athletic, American appearance who he was. Dirty Hector would have to wait.

"Señor Harris, Inspector Abaroa. I am sorry for the ... eh, em ... circumstances but I am glad you are here. I am sorry that I missed you up front. I apologize for my distraction." She stood up, swiped her wrinkled shirt downward, paused and gestured her empathy in her kind eyes and a touch on his arm.

"How was your flight?"

David wrestled for a second with the fact that Inspector Abaroa was clearly a beautiful woman. Exotic even. Wild, sunkissed blonde highlighted, curly, light brown hair, sparkling hazel eyes. He was also taken back by her appearance and like, any red-blooded male, he briefly took notice but was sobered almost instantly back to reality.

Disheveled further, David replied, "Hello Inspector, thank you, yes … it was … well … a flight. Where … where is my wife?"

"Come, I'll take you to the morgue. I know this is a very difficult time for you señor. I cannot imagine how you are feeling. Whatever I can do to help, please do not hesitate to tell me."

"You can help me find out why my wife killed herself. What … who … drove her to do this. I just can't believe that she would do it. Maybe … maybe someone did this to her."

Inspector Abaroa stepped back, cocked her head at David and looked at him quizzically, then affirmed in her own doubts of this being a suicide case.

"Let us walk Señor Harris."

David obliged, "Your English is pretty good, Ms. Abaroa."

"Please, Camila. And, yes, thank you. I studied abroad in California, briefly, while in university, and eh, my family's business, we catered to British tourists where I come from. My mother implored me to know the language."

The two continued on through the hall and navigated silently together through the busy station, down the white marble stairs to the lower level towards the morgue. Camila grabbed him firmly by the elbow and pulled him aside into a corner where no one was passing by.

"Eh, I must tell you … I understand you must be very confused … the coroner is ruling the cause of death to be, eh, suicide. But … Señor Harris … I have some … how do you say … concerns … suspicions … that I have raised with my superior."

David's heart raced. He never wanted to believe his wife killed herself but this corroboration perked his lingering suspicions. David's face became red. He was afraid. He listened intently to Inspector Camila's Spanish-accented English.

"You say that you want me to help you find out why your

wife killed herself, no? Señor David, please you must tell me anything … anything at all that might help me to understand. Why do you think that your wife may not have taken her own life?"

David, now taking shallow, fast breaths, chest heaving, fumbling over his words, "She … she … she was working on a … she worked in pharma … there, there was an issue with one of the trials, drugs … she thought that her boss might be trying to fast-track it and came here to bring falsified data to his attention."

"Your wife's … eh … company, what is it called?"

"Parax, but they are contracted with a company here in Spain, called Valencian Bioscience. Richard Blackwell is the CEO of Parax. He has been living here in Spain in the summers. He has an office, a team here in Madrid. But, my wife … I just can't picture her doing anything to harm herself over anything … even if she did something wrong at her job."

Camila's eyes widened. She knew of Valencian Bioscience, and knew that a few of the officers on the force would moonlight as security for the company. More importantly, an ex-officer and suspected murderer, Raúl Garcia had been under their employ. She also decided that now was not the time to share a piece of evidence found on the scene: a Valencian Bioscience-inscribed pocket knife.

Camila grabbed David by his arm again, this time, gently – mentioning nothing of Raúl Garcia nor the knife – and escorted David down the stairs to the morgue. "Come now, we will go to see your wife. We can talk more on this later."

David became lightheaded as he entered the cold morgue. The portly mortician greeted David with brown round eyes and bushy eyebrows and escorted him to the locker. The room was cold and tiled white. Steel tables flanked the room where fellow deceased had laid and where fresh cadavers would also soon lay. The Madrid sun still found a way in through the street level windows above, flickering light around the room.

The mortician moved smoothly and rhythmically towards the locker handle, as he had rehearsed so many times before without concern for who was contained therein. He rolled the slab out and pulled the sheet back to reveal Rebecca Harris. It was her. David's eyes rolled back and he collapsed, hitting his head on a table behind him. David passed out into blackness.

6.

David's eyes opened to an unfamiliar place. He was on a couch in what seemed to be a small apartment, furnished minimally, modernly. He sat up, rubbed his eyes and felt the throbbing on the back of his head restart, reminding him of the day before. He looked around for his phone, finding it on the coffee table next to him, placed neatly along with the rest of his belongings. It was 7 a.m. on June 20; he had slept all day and night. David got up, groggy and famished. He walked to the balcony opposite the couch, opened the doors and walked out. He was greeted with a burst of sunshine along with a wonderful smell of some sort of sweet, baked goodness wafting in to him. He was high up. He scanned the terra cotta rooftops, the makeshift antennas, the laundry lines, the cathedral peaks and the mountains in the distance. The birds were singing in unison with the clamor of traffic sounds and chatter coming from the café below. It was a pleasant scene but David's pounding head demanded that he shrug it off and turn to more odious affairs before him. Turning back to go inside, he was greeted by Camila

Abaroa, the inspector from the day before.

"How is your head, Mr. Harris?" she asked.

"Please, call me David. And, throbbing,"

"Would you like some café?"

"That would be tremendous. Do you have any aspirin or Tylenol? Where … where am I?"

"Yes, of course. I hope it's okay that I brought you here to my flat. I didn't … I didn't know where you were staying or if you had made any arrangements. And besides … I … I thought it might be safer for you if I kept you close by," Camila shared apprehensively.

"It's fine … it's fine … it's … wait … why did you say 'safer'? Am I in some kind of trouble … why do I need to be safe?" David began to grow frustrated from his confusion.

"David, please, let us sit and have some café. I will explain," Camila said, already in her pressed uniform. She escorted David to the little table and small chairs on the balcony with the incredible view. She poured him a cup of Spanish style café con leche and sat down with him.

"It's very … how do you say, eh … complicated. Why don't you tell me about your wife first? You had mentioned that you had suspicions, yesterday in the precinct. Tell me about those suspicions, David."

Dazed by the potential corroboration and the pain from the knot on his head, David's eyes wandered around the vista. His head was ringing. He scanned the back log of files in his mind, recalling all that had happened in the last three days. David always had trouble focusing, perhaps from undiagnosed ADHD, but his mental clarity was becoming sharper with his newfound purpose. He was going to find his why his wife was dead now – he knew it.

"I don't know where to start. There's ... there's a lot to tell. Rebecca ... my, my wife, she was..." David became choked up and the tears began to stream.

"It's okay, David, let it out. You need time to grieve. Let's take a break and you go take a rest," the Detective said in a calming and relaxing tone.

"No, no, just give me a minute. I'll be alright ... I need to get it out, I need to tell someone before I lose it all."

David took a deep breath, wiped his tears and continued, "As I told you yesterday, Rebecca works for Parax ... uh, *worked*, for Parax ... a CRO — it's one of those companies that facilitates the testing of drugs for Pharma companies, like a middle man — and was working on a contract for Valencian Bioscience. I know that there was some issue, some discrepancy. She was frustrated and had told me at one point that her CEO, Richard Blackwell, and her counterpart at Valencian, Ana Esperanza, were pushing to have a contract on some new product fast-tracked. I never trusted Richard. I am not versed in all the pharmaceutical lingo but I have picked up enough from Rebecca to get an idea of how things work. And something was fishy about the arrangement with Valencian Bioscience. That I do know. It pissed Rebecca off to no end. She was a stickler for details and they were always trying to get one over. Richard bought a house in Valencia when Parax first contracted with Valencian Bioscience. That raised Rebecca's concern, initially. There was nothing illegal, but it didn't sit well with Rebecca – it seemed suspicious to her for some reason. I don't know what it all means or if there's something there but I just ... I just know that somehow, this is all tied to why Rebecca is dead. It's the only reason that makes sense to me. Please, Ms. Abaroa, tell me something."

Camila Abaroa's senses were tingling. The ever-diligent detective was putting puzzle pieces together in her mind as she listened intently to David. Neglecting her civic duty to keep evidence and information confidential during an ongoing investigation, Camila decided to share with David about the case, even if it meant her career. There was too much coming together. She felt compelled to tell him. She was drawn to David's earnestness and conviction. She empathized with that fact that he lost his wife. She saw the truth in his eyes, the love he had for his wife and the pain he was now facing.

"There, there is, well, eh, something I should *not* tell you, David. But I feel as though I must. The day of your wife's ... em ... untimely demise, we were at the scene and I found something peculiar there. There was knife under the bed. It was a small pocketknife. Eh, um ... señor Harris ... on that knife was inscribed ... it ... it said ... 'Valencian Bioscience'."

David drew back.

"What ... what ... what do you mean?" David sheepishly asked. "That's the company Rebecca's company was working with that I'm talking about. Maybe she had it as a gift from them in her purse ... or ... or they gave it to her?"

"Es, well, yes, it is possible the pocketknife was hers, yes. But tell me Mr. David, do you think your wife would've had this pocketknife?"

"No, there's no way ... *I don't think*," David pensively replied.

David paused in thought. "Wait a minute ... I helped pack her bags. I've never even seen her hold a pocket knife, let alone actually have one. I mean, she just started working with Valencian last year ... we haven't been back here to Spain to visit since after she started working with them. And I know that she came straight from the airport to the hotel here when she arrived. I spoke with her on the phone, so I know she had no time to visit their office yet. I suppose they could've handed her one in the car, but that doesn't make sense either. Richard drove her and he's with Parax, not Valencian." David's face grew red.

"Well, it is something ... something didn't feel right

60

about it being in her room. It seemed strange for it to be under the bed. And ... I do know someone who also works for Valencian. And I will tell you something else. The way in which she had hanged herself. It did not, eh, make sense to me. There was nothing giving her leverage to get her above the bed ... no chair, no stool. Tell me Mr. David, was your wife an athlete of some kind? Judging by the looks of how she got up to the light fixture, she would have had an extraordinary athletic ability to jump that high to get herself into position to ... eh ... you know," Camila said.

"No. Ms. Abaroa. *Camila.* She was not an *athlete.* If there is something you are not telling me, you need to do so. You are telling me there was a knife that wasn't hers, with 'Valencian Bioscience' written on it and that she physically could not of ... hung herself, by herself ... what do we do? What else do you know? Who do *you* know that works for Valencian? What are you trying to tell me?"

Camila could see indignation rising in David and interjected, "Mr. David, please, I will tell you everything I know and what my ... em ... suspicions are. You need to understand that my career is on the line by even having you here in my home. An open investigation into a suicide with suspicious details and the widower of the deceased staying in my home. You must know that it cannot look good and that you cannot repeat any of the information that I am sharing with you. Tell me. Tell me you understand."

"I do ... I do ... I just ... if my wife didn't actually hang herself then I am going to..."

Camila interjected again, "I understand your grief and your need to know. That's why I brought you here ... to talk. Now, what I am about to tell you is strictly off the record and confidential. Mr. Harris, I have left the case open and have committed to my chief that this is a possible homicide. The reason, besides the suspicious scene of death, was that upon review of the hotel's video security tapes, I noticed someone who I know, entering and exiting the hotel lobby at around the approximate time of your wife's demise. The camera in her hall did not capture anyone entering or exiting her room, other than her. However, the camera pans every two minutes between her hall and the adjacent one and I caught enough of a glimpse of this person. What raised my concern, David, was *who* this man was. He … he is not a good man."

"Who is it? You tell me right now…" David shouted.

"David, this man is very, very peligroso … em … dangerous. His name is Raúl Garcia. He was formerly an inspector for the department here in Madrid. It was a few years ago now that he was acquitted, and subsequently fired, for abusing a suspect in a murder investigation. He was also suspected of murdering some homeless young men and a prostitute. The witness who was to testify against Raúl abusing the suspect never appeared at the court. Raúl was let go. And because of the media stories surrounding the case, he was quietly dismissed and never had to serve time for allegedly abusing the suspect. There was too much negative attention for our department and ever since, we have been keeping tabs on Mr. Garcia. He has been working as a private security detail for several companies, and getting fired from those jobs in short order. Now, he is employed again … this time with none other than … Valencian Bioscience."

David's eyes possessed a glazed over, psychotic quality, fixed on the window behind Camila and in a calm, monotone change of voice he simply replied, "Well, then that's where we start."

Camila never broke protocols and always played by the book. She began to question if trusting her instinct to bring David to her apartment was a mistake. She had never made a mistake in her detective work before but her instinct was now driving her decisions about David.

"You can stay here as long as you need Mr. Harris. I have to go to work for a couple of hours. I will leave a key for you. Come and go as you need. Here is my mobile number," Camila handed him a card, "Just try to stay out of trouble."

David agreed and Camila walked out the door to continue her investigation into Rebecca's death. On her way to her office, she visited the hotel that Rebecca was found dead in one more time to talk to the concierge that had been on duty. That same concierge had just quit once the police first came to the scene. Now, the management was less than forthcoming about the day in question and Camila ordered them in for an interrogation later that afternoon.

Camila left the hotel wondering about Rebecca and David. She had never had another man in her apartment but she trusted David and stifled the physical attraction she felt for him. It wouldn't look good if anyone knew that he was there.

David sat on her white leather for couch for what felt like seconds but turned out to be two hours, staring, pondering. Then he remembered Ana. He began searching for Ana's contact and a local number for the Valencian office on his phone. It took some time but finally he found a number.

Two rings and a receptionist answered. Ana Esperanza was unavailable. The receptionist sounded emotional.

"Could you just let her know that David Harris called. It's about her colleague, Rebecca Harris, my wife. Something has happened. It's urgent that I speak to her."

The receptionist gasped, "Sí, uh yes sir, I will let her know."

"Please, take my number down."

David was unsettled by the brief conversation. He pulled himself up, took a shower in Camila's blue-tiled shower, smelling her shampoo bottle and feeling guilty for doing so, and got dressed.

Plugging the address into his phone, he walked down the stairs of Camila's walk-up in a blur and down the craggy, cobblestone alleyway. It was siesta time and few things were open. All David could think about was Rebecca's body lying there. Over and over, it played in his mind. He pictured her hanging in the hotel. He let the idea of her demise as intentional, creep in. He envisioned someone handling her, touching his wife's body. He felt like a rabid dog, his mind racing, raging.

After walking for an hour in the hot afternoon sun, David needed a break. He didn't stop to look around up until this point. He was blind with single-mindedness to get to Ana. Her office was on the other side of the city from Camila's apartment but David opted to walk, forgetting about the heat that can radiate Madrid in the summer.

Full of restaurants, Madrid's best ones tended to be out-of-the-way, hole-in-the-wall niche, boutique spots. An aroma enchanted his senses as he walked, and reminded him that he hadn't eaten in over 24 hours. He looked down the alley that seemed to be bustling and took note of the restaurant creating the rabble. Ducking down the low overhead, into the basement-entry restaurant, David found what seemed like a bootleg taco joint. Hipsters with ridiculous tattoos and maidens with blue and pink hair eyeballed the stranger. How dare he find their restaurant?

Sitting down amidst the creatures, beaded door curtains, kitschy pop art and mismatched tables and chairs, David breathed a sigh of relaxation seeing they had Dos Equis on tap. A reprieve with the familiar beer would help calm him down. He couldn't care less of what the other customers thought of him right now. In years prior, he would've been so nervous, he wouldn't have even entered such an establishment. He believed that he sucked the cool out of any room despite his good looks and unique ethnicity. Being self-conscious can be a good thing. For David, it was a detriment and prevented him from engaging people. He had been far too concerned about others judging him that he simply did nothing and went nowhere that would leave him exposed.

The air conditioning was heavenly and the smell coming from the kitchen even more so. David considered himself an aficionado of authentic Central American cuisine. This wasn't it. This was a hybrid. It was Molecular gastronomy meets Mexican-inspired flavors. The strange combination of flavors satiated David, though only for a fleeting moment. One of the only ways Rebecca was able to coerce David into going out with friends lately was under the guise of trying a new restaurant.

Sloshing down the last of his beer, David threw his payment on the table and darted for the door. It was lost time but worth it. Despite the cultural faux pas, he tipped the blue-haired, tattooed waitress generously for her rapid delivery of rations. She watched him leave the restaurant, perplexed, as if they had just been patronized by a ghost.

Valencian Bioscience was close. The imposing building stood out with its postmodern architecture — strange in contrast to its neighboring buildings. Armed security guards flanked the entrance and David could see more of them inside. Security cameras covered every angle. Why did a pharmaceutical company need so much security? Sure there are probably desirable compounds within its walls but not worth this much muscle, David thought. Approaching the building, two men rushed towards David, speaking unintelligible Spanish and pointing their fingers. One of them put their hand on his chest.

"I'm here to visit Ana Esperanza. My wife worked with you guys. Calm down, fellas."

One of the men spoke Spanish into his headset. He looked at the other guard and shook his head.

"Ana no es here. You need to leave señor."

"What the hell? I'm just here to see someone that works

here. I don't understand."

The security guard simply pointed his index finger to the street motioning David to get off of their property. Then he flashed his Glock on his hip.

"Okay, okay. Just tell Ana Esperanza that David Harris came to see her. She knows who I am. My wife worked with her and now she's dead. My wife talked to Ana about me before. I know she knows me."

Another index finger pointed without a word.

David admitted defeat and turned to walk away, stopping only to turn and flip them the bird from across the street. He knew that encounter did not feel right. Why on earth would they not let him into the building and why would they need that much security, he wondered.

It was evening time and David had a long walk ahead of him back to Camila's apartment. David soaked in the sounds and sights of the city. The honking horns, the rapid-fire Castilian. People clamored into tapas bars and into side street cafés, smoking cigarettes, drinking Rioja and Sangria. The centuries old buildings, newly paved major thoroughfares, royal embellishments and grime made for an anarchistic aesthetic that somehow flowed seamlessly together. The Spanish people walk fast and talk fast — and that was just it — they were going to go about their life no matter what was going on or being built around them. The tourists just looked lost and stood out like sore thumbs. And much like Times Square in New York, Plaza Sol held the bulk of them. As David walked through the swelling crowds, he kept his hand on the outline of his wallet in his front pocket. This was a sucker's square. David walked with purpose and without consulting a mapping system through the rabble. He felt like someone was following him.

David found Camila's neighborhood easily. Her apartment building was another story. It was a confusing layout and he was mentally and physically fatigued by the time he made it back to the vicinity. Jet lag was hammering him. He didn't want to concede to the city by calling Camila but he relented, pulling her card out to call for help finding the building.

"I'll meet you, I know where you are," Camila assured him upon his distress call.

David sat down on the stone stoop of a cathedral. David hated waiting and he hated admitting defeat even more. He pictured Rebecca's dead body and he felt helpless. Just as he was about to sob, yet again, at the uselessness he felt, he saw Camila bouncing around the corner. She smiled and waved at him excitedly. She had been anxious to know where he was and where had been during the day. She had become worried about him in the last hour.

"That was fast. I am so sorry I got lost. I guess I just got turned around or something."

"It is no problem, Mr. Harris. You almost made it. I am just there around the corner," Camila said with a smile, pointing.

"I've spent some time here and I know where most things are. But your neighborhood ... I've never really been over here."

"Yes, it's a small district," Camila changed subjects, "So, what did you get up to today?"

"Oh, not a whole lot. Just tried to visit Valencian Bioscience to ask why my wife is dead. Didn't make it to the front door. I tried to connect with Ana but I couldn't even get past the security guards. Something is up. It was really strange."

"You went to Valencian? Without me? David, *please*, I know you want to help, but you can't interfere. These security persons — they are very dangerous people. You need to lay low now. Let me do my job."

"I'm sorry. I'm sorry, Camila. I understand. I just..."

"Come, let us go. I am sure you are hungry. I have food at the apartamento."

The half-block walk back to her apartment was a shameful one for David. He was embarrassed for not finding it by himself—the way a real man would.

Sitting down at her modest table for two on her veranda, Camila served up a local soup of fideos and chorizo. It was a smoky, meaty soup, savory and perfect despite the heat of the day still wafting into the nighttime air. It was her version of soul food.

"This is amazing. Did you make this?"

"Yes, it was my mother's recipe. It's good when *you* don't feel so good."

"Kind of like a better chicken noodle soup."

"We should talk about the case. But I'm sure you must be tired."

"I'm exhausted. Can we talk in the morning?"

"Of course, get some rest," Camila cleaned up their bowls and looked through folders as David retired again on the couch.

7.

Valencian Bioscience Office, Madrid, Spain, 20 June 8:15 a.m. CET

Ana Esperanza's terse lips rarely cracked a smile. She was a driven, hard-nosed working-class Spaniard. Her lips broke, faintly resembling a vein of contentment when she sat down in her less than modest cubicle on this day, however. Ana had decided to treat herself to her childhood favorite on the way to work – churros con chocolaté. Having carved out a few extra minutes before getting on the train to work, she stopped at her local churro bar. It was a small luxury after an unusually pressure-filled last few weeks. The smell wafted through her office when she had walked in earlier, alerting the nostrils of her jealous coworkers.

It had been far too long that she sat in this same desk. She never asked for a new office but she knew she deserved it and so did her superior, Ahmed Bahl. He was a Pakistani national whose fluency in English, Spanish and German, and his backstabbing, claw-his-the-way-to-the-top bravado earned him a one way ticket to the Global Head Chair of Valencian Bioscience. He was ruthless and Ana was a willing subject if it meant earning enough to get out of her parents' cramped Madrid apartment. As the Director of Procurement for Valencian Bioscience, she was always under pressure to make sure their drugs were processed through the clinical trial phases on time and under budget.

She sat down and took a deep breath. As she dipped the churro into the chocolaté, she smiled wide for once at that cramped desk. She opened her laptop and girded herself up for what she believed was going to be a confrontational day with her American counterpart and sometime nemesis, Rebecca Harris. She liked Rebecca. She always had. She was tough and stood her ground. They would have to fight against each other from time to time, however, in order to accomplish their individual companies' goals – and today would be another one of those days. She was a pushy Spaniard but she meant well. Ana expected Rebecca to come breezing into the office at any minute. Rebecca had flown over from the U.S. specifically to meet with her. Ana knew that despite knowing that she had been up to no good, had to act as if Rebecca was crazy and wrong. That's what Ahmed had instructed her to do, anyway. Always put the company first, even if it meant lying. Out of fear of reprisal in the form of public castigation, Ana always did as she was told. Ahmed was merciless when it came to rebuking his employees and their attrition rate was abnormally high as a result.

Ana looked at the postmodern clock on her desk and wondered where Rebecca was. She was now 10 minutes late. Rebecca wouldn't be late for this. She wouldn't even be late for a pre-dawn TransAtlantic conference call. She reviewed the text message that she had received from Rebecca earlier to to confirm that she was in-fact in Madrid, but never responded to, out of a lack of a decent response:

"Ana, I'm here. And we need to talk about Ahmed and Richard — something is up. We need to talk off record when we meet. I know we've had our issues and I believe you are only doing what you are told but you and I both know the validity of RXG1 is questionable, at best. See you soon."

Ana's senses wavered. She sat nervously in preparation for the encounter but knew she had to conceal her true feelings. She repositioned her gaze to the bolded, emails coming into her inbox – one marked "Urgent", as most of them are marked, even if they are not, in-fact, urgent:

"...we are saddened by the loss of our colleague and friend, Rebecca Harris. Please consult your HR team if you need assistance with grief counseling. Sincerely, Richard Blackwell, CEO Parax."

That's all Ana needed to read from this urgent email for her heart to start pounding, head to start spinning and tears to well up in her eyes. Ana read through the disingenuous email and knew the callous intent — go cry and hurry up and get back to work. She retreated swiftly to the women's restroom past Ahmed's office and his leering eyes. Springing through the door, Ana collapsed to her knees and began to sob.

"Cálmate Ana," she thought aloud to herself.

Ana had just spoken on the phone to Rebecca days before. And now? She's dead? Ana couldn't believe it. It was true they had their battles but Ana's respect for Rebecca never faltered. Maybe a line crossed, verbally, here and there but Ana was an impassioned Madrileño. She cursed, she talked with her hands and she had an attitude. But that didn't mean she didn't care about people. More than being upset her colleague, Ana began to realize that her emotions were actually more rooted in fear for her own life. Rebecca's text message only compounded the dread.

Ana had been coerced by Ahmed to push things through

on more than one occasion. To fib a little, here and there, to get the wheels greased. After all, their drugs were "saving the world"; at least that's what she had been indoctrinated to believe. Ana knew that what she was doing was wrong but had hoped, much like Rebecca, by some measure, that it would net a positive result for a patient somewhere. Regardless, she didn't have much of a choice. Her ailing mother relied on Ana's income and there were no other job options that could pay her that well.

Ahmed was emotionless, ruthless; a surgical tactician when it came to negotiation. He was also an intimidating mentor to Ana. She had to produce results for Ahmed – faster than on time and cheaper than under budget. For the last several months, she had been pressed harder than ever before by an especially ornery and cold Ahmed to do whatever she could to fast track their cancer drug. This was the latest source of friction between Ana and Rebecca, whose company, Parax, was facilitating the testing for a new cancer drug to be released — RXG1. Ana had been especially rough with Rebecca lately, as instructed by Ahmed. And it was the reason for Rebecca's, now permanently delayed visit. Ana had fudged a few details about RXG1 – also instructed by Ahmed.

The press had been particularly kind to Valencian Biosciences as news trickled out about their potentially life-saving treatment in RXG1. Ana knew better though. RXG1 was Ahmed's baby and he held it close to his chest. Ana could see that things were not adding up with the compound — RXG1 had accelerated through the trials despite the interim statistical analysis indicating that the compound was not achieving the primary endpoint. But, inevitably, those finite details were of little consequence to her, as she was too afraid of Ahmed to not do as exactly as instructed. Ahmed wined and dined a few of his various connections at the well-established news organizations, leaking some of the more fantastical and favorable details of their trial results. Ana had even prepared lines for Ahmed to feed to them prior to their meetings. "All part of the process of saving lives, Ana," he would tell her. Ana understood there was more money on the line than ever before in the history of Valencian Biosciences. They had invested everything into RXG1.

Human life was less than a commodity to Ahmed. He was raised into a cruel existence. He watched his prostitute mother return home daily with fresh bruises and cuts and witnessed the murder of his older brother when he was just a young boy on the streets of Karachi. He knew at an early age that he had to take whatever he could, however he could, out of this life. He studied hard knowing that he didn't want to die on the streets of Karachi like Aahil.

Ahmed set his sights on the USA as an escape. Most of his fellow Pakistani friends tried to go to the U.K. Ahmed, however, had the hubris to believe that he could become famous and rich and believed the USA to be the ultimate symbol of having 'made it'. After hustling his way to America, having earned enough money through street cons and a couple of robberies to buy a ticket, he landed in New York City. He was immediately poorer than he was in Pakistan. There was no way he would end up a cab driver and he wouldn't be a street vendor. He refused to settle for minimum wage, despite it being far more than he would have earned back home. He was 17 and began doing his research on where the least expensive places to live with the best universities were. North Carolina. He could live for a fraction of what he was paying for to live in squalor in the city. Working odd jobs and committing a few petty thefts he saved enough to buy a bus ticket. After doing some research, he figured out a way to manipulate the University of North Carolina's admission protocols. As a foreign national, he was able to sell himself as added diversity to the registrar. Ahmed discovered that he had a gift; he was a master manipulator.

Ahmed soon became enamored with the sophisticated southern aristocratic, old-money lifestyle. It became his drive to someday live like those white people did. Ahmed was intelligent, but also had street-wise senses and knew how to both move up the corporate ladder when he landed his first Business Development role at a small pharmaceutical firm there in North Carolina while he was working two other jobs and maintaining his grades. He also figured out how to cut corners where he knew he wouldn't get caught. With the assistance from his roommate there at UNC, they would decide to take the pharmaceutical industry by storm.

Now in his 50s, and after a couple of decades in the industry, Ahmed had moved internationally several times to finally land a CEO spot at the burgeoning Valencian Biosciences. It was a small fish, but Ahmed trusted his ability to manipulate and position the company for rapid growth and expansion: Cancer. Cancer was always a risky endeavor, financially, for pharma companies. The results just weren't there. That didn't matter to Ahmed though, he had a plan. Together, with his old college roommate they would do whatever it took to see their plan through that they began devising all those years ago. And that college roommate and cohort was expected in the Valencian Bioscience office any minute now.

Ana was reeling as she sorted herself out. She adjusted her skirt clinging to her petite frame, flung her dark black long wavy hair back, returned to her cubicle and sat down at her desk. She pondered alone to herself, staring off into the distance. Would it be possible that something nefarious happened to Rebecca? Would Ahmed really be capable of orchestrating something like this? She looked toward his office and saw his figure staring back in her direction. '*Si, por supuesto ... yes, of course he would,*' she thought.

She knew Ahmed's needling was not simply for the best interest of the company, nor even for a love of money. Ana knew Ahmed's story, his childhood. She had seen how he treated her fellow obsequious co-workers in the office and had even witnessed some of his more unsavory dealings with blonde, Eastern European immigrant prostitutes that hung around Gran Via after hours. The latter would not have been seen by Ana, had she not been working late for Ahmed — she missed the last Metro to her stop, forcing her to walk to the next connecting Metro station. She was nervous when she caught a glimpse of her inebriated boss flirting with, and then violently grabbing, one of the girls that night. She hid in the shadows watching the encounter and the dirty business transpire – it made her stomach turn. No, she knew that Ahmed was an evil man even without these witnessed encounters. She had a sixth sense about him and it made her spine tingle when she thought of Rebecca.

Still staring blankly into the distance, a male figure took shape in her gaze. Well built, his hair silver, eyes blue. Handsome. He whisked into her cubicle, "Hello, my darling Ana, how are you?" the figure said in a charming southern drawl. It was a visit from Richard Blackwell, CEO of Parax in an unusually chipper mood given the breaking news of Rebecca. All of this would have been far less disconcerting if she hadn't received that text from Rebecca sent from her hotel here in Madrid — and that she was on to RXG1.

She mustered a plasticine smile, "Buenos dias, Richard. Ahmed is waiting for you."

8.

David's head lifted off the pillow with only a faint throbbing from the two days before when he cracked his head on the table in the morgue. He sat up in the guest bed in the loft of Camila's apartment. He had graduated from the couch to her guest space but didn't remember leaving the couch. He could hear Camila's shower going in her one bathroom. He got up and looked around the apartment from the loft above. Pictures of Camila on the beach, on a boat, with a surfboard — yet with no man — hung from her stark white walls. His eyes were unable to focus and catch them the day before.

He slinked his tall body down the winding, narrow staircase to the main floor.

"Ah, good morning, David," Camila startled David in her towel. "I will get dressed and we can go get some café. Do you you need to shower?"

David's hair tussled and cheeks flushed, "Uh … no, I'll be alright. Coffee sounds great. I'll be ready when you are."

"Great, we can pick up our conversation about Rebecca, Parax, Valencian, Raúl, everything, okay?"

David nodded, blushing further at her appearance.

After a few moments of shuffling, Camila emerged clothed in white capri jeans and a silky top, ready to hit the streets. Camila and David exited her modest, yet modern and well-appointed apartment in search of answers. After walking down the long, winding stairs, David thought to himself, *'Don't they have elevators here?'* The pair exited into into the hot sun, now glazing the cobblestone Madrid street below. David's eye's adjusted and drew in the vibrancy he missed the day before. A couple of school-aged kids kicking a soccer ball to each other, occasionally bouncing it off the bill-plastered wall full of political advertisements now smattered in graffiti. A little old lady inefficiently dragged a cart with groceries up the hilly street, across those hot cobblestones. These carts seemed to be employed generously here, yet to little efficacy.

The narrow road seemed impassable by car, however, a small passenger bus honked as it turned the corner down the road, barely scraping through the impossible passage, causing the boys to stop their game of soccer and hug a wall of one of the many crammed buildings. Most of the buildings were apartments, fitted with a tiny tapas bar on the first floor. A series of brooms flickered out of the doors of these tapas bars lining the street, absolving the prior night's revelry that only jostled David's slumber once, around 2 a.m. Legs of cured ham, known as Jamón Ibérico, were being displayed in the entrances of the bars. A café, busy with smokers sitting and soaking up the warm rays across the plaza from a cathedral, the same one David gave up at the evening prior, now chiming its 9 o'clock bells, was buzzing.

A stylishly dressed gentleman with a lithe physique, adorned in classic garb ala Havana, circa 1958, stood on the corner across the street reading *EL PAÍS*, the local newspaper, with a long, burning cigarette in-between his fingers. Several expired butts were at his feet. David glanced at him again and their eyes met. The birds chirped loudly overhead. This man was out of place. David and Camila walked in the opposite direction towards Plaza Mayor.

David was an impeccable judge of character – it was one of the attributes that first attracted Rebecca. It never seemed to work out in David's favor when it came to making business decisions but it was as clear as a bell that the man looking at David and Camila had a malicious intent. David's casual stride picked up to a faster pace, dragging Camila along with him.

"I think we've got some company, Camila," David said, looking over his shoulder to discover the well-dressed, handsome man no longer cared about the day's news, finding something more interesting in David and Camila. The two navigated through the crooked streets utilizing Camila's local knowledge of shortcuts to get them to a more populated section. La Latina was only a 10-minute walk to the city's center but it felt like an eternity as she passed through her usual haunts.

By the time they made it to Mercado San Miguel, a historic, large, central marketplace where one could procure anything from fresh oysters and manchego to a nice bottle of Rioja and alcaparras, the man had gained on the two fast friends. David remembered how busy the market could be from one of his trips with Rebecca – they had spent all day in that same market, ogling at the overpriced delicacies, bouncing between vendors and sampling everything exotic they could find. He knew that they could give Mr. Handsome the slip amongst the crowd. Camila nodded in agreement as David pointed to the market.

David began to dart across the busy cobblestone street, instinctually grabbing Camila's hand to speed up the process. Madrileños were always pushy in crowds so as the two escapees nudged, squeezed and slithered through the busy morning crowd, it went unnoticed.

"Duck down," David ordered Camila.

"Que es, duck?" she replied.

"¡Tu cabeza, abajo, ya!" David insisted as he yanked Camila behind a cheese vendor's stall. They crouched as their pursuer wantonly hurriedly passed by, scanning for them. They looked at each other and slinked back the way they came, out the glass front doors, across the same cobblestone street and into the open safety of Plaza Mayor. Their hearts raced.

"What is going on, Camila? Why was that man chasing us?" David, out of breath, adrenaline now ebbing, asked the red-faced Camila as they hid, propping themselves up on an exterior step to the mercado.

David, becoming nearly hysterical, "I told you ... I knew ... I knew that Rebecca did not kill herself. But why would some random stranger, or mugger or rapist or even a serial killer stage it to look like she killed herself? It's not right. It doesn't make sense. The only thing that makes sense to me now is that someone who wanted to shut her up or for her to disappear would've done this. This guy that's chasing us ... he's part of it somehow, isn't he?"

Camila bent over, caught her breath and explained, "David. The man I spoke of earlier, yesterday morning ... Raúl Garcia ... I believe that is one of his cronies. We always suspected Raúl was dirty and a killer but he's developed his own little network ... well ... gang. If there was any doubt that Raúl had something to do with your wife, I am now fairly certain that he was involved on some level."

David replied acrimoniously, "Well, let's find h..." David's words were suddenly interrupted by the screeching of tires on the cobblestone street adjacent to where they were standing in the plaza. It was a black Mercedes, though David didn't know what model – Rebecca always knew more about cars than he did. Two large men in nice slacks and short-sleeved dress shirts and tattoos started jogging briskly in their direction, oblivious to the congestion of tourists.

"I think we better move, Camila," David's eyes darted around for an exit.

"There!" Camila pointed towards the exit across the plaza towards Centro, the center of the city. The two ran across, disturbing the pigeons, fluttering them frantically above the café patrons and onlookers sipping their mid-morning expressos. Running through the exit, a small latino man, most likely from El Salvador or Venezuela, with half of a bootlegged fuzzy, red Elmo costume was dressing for the day's swindles. His eyes met David's in a split-second of mutual déjà vu.

Another Mercedes screeched up, this time it was silver, nearly blocking their exit. Running around the car, there were now five, well-dressed men chasing them across the city. Camila and David were now sprinting for their lives. The congested city was on their side, however. Droves of tourists idled aimlessly in Puerta del Sol again, looking fruitlessly at maps, at their phones and at the other hopelessly turned-around visitors. It was very hot now. Higher-end shops that lined the streets occasionally misted water vapor, air conditioning, and overbearing designer fragrances out into the street, enticing wayward respite seekers. David wasn't a stranger to the benefits of the charms of the free mist and air conditioning. They ducked into the El Corte Ingles young men's section at street level — a multi-level mall — and received a blast to their senses of their latest fragrance, house music beats and ice-cold air. The two entrance-exit points were on opposite sides of the building. In one, up the escalators and out the other. It wasn't enough. They still had a tail chasing behind them through the store and out the opposite end.

Back through the plaza. The crowd would be their last-ditch attempt. The amalgam of chaotic, wandering bodies would produce enough of a cover for Camila and David to once again slip through the constricting grasp of what they now believed to be the orchestration of Raúl Garcia or someone pulling his strings.

Hand-in-hand, darting through the sea of humanity, David and Camila blended in as if they were running to their next metro stop, garnering no second looks as they frantically navigated their escape. As they passed the alleyway in front of Chocolatería San Ginés, David's nose picked up the enchanting waft of wonderful and decadent chocolaté con churros — the world famous chocolate stop was a just off a busy tourist paseo and hard to find. It was only a split second distraction when, suddenly, he felt the force of a man spearing him from the waist, down to the hard cobblestone ground.

The melee attracted little notice as they landed in the narrow passageway. Besides, homeless men, prostitutes and panhandlers aired their grievances in the middle of busy Madrid tourist hot spots all of the time, and they occasionally ended in physical altercations. It wasn't an uncommon sight. David's instinctual reaction was to get up and run but he was pinned. One of the finely dressed men had taken David to the ground and now appeared to be far more muscular and clearly versed in brawling.

David, now in a chokehold, blinked as he gasped for air and envisioned his widow. For a brief moment, David thought of letting go, until the vision of his deceased bride gently appeared to his fading consciousness, almost as if to tell David his time was not up. He began to feel a sensation of a will to fight again. But it was too late, the weight of the assailant collapsed on top of David in a thud of human meat. David's hero focused into vision. The well-dressed thug underestimated Detective Abaroa's now-apparent collusion. Camila had cracked the man over the head with her collapsible baton — a sure and sturdy weapon for any woman on the job.

"We need to get out of here – *now!*" Camila said. "There will be police here soon."

"Aren't *you* a cop?" David retorted, groggy.

"Right now I am helping you. I don't know what that makes me. Now, get up!" Camila grabbed David's hand and pulled him up.

David, embarrassed, got up and attempted to shake off the encounter. He saw stars and was angry from not being able to reciprocate during the engagement. He kicked the fallen man in the ribs. He didn't make a sound. It lacked the gratification David expected.

"Are you done?! Let's go!"

Appearing as if they might be completing a light morning jog — David's skinned knee, sore hip and blood on his shirt notwithstanding — the pair came to a stop after coming upon an open space. Camila and David caught their breath and spun 360 degrees assessing the square they now found themselves in. They were in Plaza de Oriente, facing the Palace. There were castle guards in front, a few lazy strollers, a lone violinist playing for change, Asian masseuses offering illegal street massages, some patrons in the café behind them and various people sitting on benches, laying on the grass, and taking pictures of the fountains and the Teatro Real. They assessed their locale and decided they could find a shady spot under a tree and figure out their next plan.

"So, are you now going to explain to me what the hell is going on?" David lambasted.

"It's … it's a lot. Come, sit. We can take an early siesta under this tree." Camila replied.

Had it not been for their circumstances, the setting was serene, elegant — romantic even. David calmed enough to look around and took in the pristine palace and beautiful surrounding park, "I haven't been to this part of the city in years. I forgot how nice it was on this side of the city." David felt like a fool for the remark in the midst of their current predicament. He always found himself making out-of-context remarks in precarious situations. It was a nervous tick that he couldn't escape. Camila tilted her head at David quizzically.

"Forget it. Tell me. Tell me everything you know."

"So, it goes back to Raúl Garcia's tenure as a police officer, aqui ... here, in Madrid. From the beginning, there were warning signs. His temper, the way he treated other officers, the way he handled criminals; there was something I could not put my finger on but I did not ever trust him. As he moved up the ranks to detective, which he should have never been able to, there were questionable methods, poor detective work, battered suspects, the list goes on. Yet, somehow, he managed to maintain his career. Things got worse, though. I can't accuse him of this for sure, but you have to understand, there was no other explanation. You see, over the last two years, there have been a series of unsolved murders. They were all street kids, homeless men, panhandlers, some even our own ears and eyes on the ground ... witnesses, eh, you call them informants, maybe? Well, a few turned up strangled, stabbed, beaten ... dead. There was a rumor that emerged among them that there was a policeman committing these acts ... fingers began pointing at Raúl."

"How did he even get that far as a cop? That would never fly in the U.S."

"No one would ever come forward to file a complaint or bear witness. They were too afraid. They all knew though. I knew. I helped get him removed from the Guardia and I've had to watch my back ever since."

"How did you get him fired?"

"There was a break-in and murder in one of the nicer areas of the city. It was all over the news as this was a prominent citizen who was killed. We were all under heavy pressure to solve this crime. Raúl saw it as an opportunity. We struggled to find any leads. Raúl, however, claimed he cracked it. He marched a young man – one of these street urchins – into the interrogation room. He was beaten, bloody. Raúl had forced a confession for the crime from him. All of a sudden, he began receiving accolades. That is until the young man's wealthy mother showed up and the boy recanted. It turned out that his mother was a well-known aristocrat with connections to the administration and the king, and despite her best intentions with schooling for the young man, he became addicted to heroin and ended up on the streets of Madrid. Not a savory person to be sure, but no killer — this his mother was sure of. Before we knew it, the papers got wind of the police abusing a suspect and the case was dropped. Raúl had to be fired despite someone higher up fighting for him to keep his job. His sloppy police work is what caught up to him. No newspapers continued to research the story however, and, in the end, Raúl quietly was dismissed and walked free. He's still out there. Now we have a string of unsolved murders of the same caliber. I know it's him. Then, your wife ..."

Camila paused, the birds chirping, distance café chatter and the sound of the wind ruffling the leaves overhead filled the silence. David looked at her contemplatively and began biting his nails as she continued.

"Did the break-in and murder of the rich person ever get solved?"

"No."

Camila continued, "It was not long after being dismissed from the police that Raúl found odd security jobs. Eventually ... eventually, he began working for Parax. There are many former police personnel working on the security team for Parax actually, which ... well ... seems odd considering they are a pharmaceutical company. I believe the CEO uses them at his compound in Valencia, privately as well."

Camila looked at David in his eyes, "You see, David, if Raúl's compatriots are following us, then..."

"Then Raul had to be involved. And if his guys who work security with him for Valenian are chasing us, then... Then, Valencian has to be involved," David interjected, looking away from the revelation.

Camila continued, "Sí, and then, well, then, there is the security camera footage of Raúl exiting your wife's hotel around the time we suspect her time of expiration. It most likely didn't help us that Raúl lives in the same neighborhood as I."

David's face was red, and hot. The rage came slowly but manifested itself differently than it had ever before. It was crystalline. Resolute. He had a channel to focus his volcanic flow. There was only one thing that his enraged mind focused on — killing Raúl Garcia. If he had left the hotel at the time of his wife's death then David needed no other proof. He was short-fused and tempestuous. David had already sealed Raúl's fate. He had already resolved to be judge, jury and executioner.

David's attempt to conceal his raw emotion was in vain. Camila read his eyes, a gift passed down from her mother. "David, we are going to catch Raúl, if he is in-fact, responsible. And anyone at Valencian. I promise you. But we have to do it the right way, my way. You Americans always must be a hero. A cowboy. You can't do anything rash here. It does not work that way in España."

David said nothing. Only malevolence showed in his eyes.

Camila looked down, resolving that there was only one thing they could do, "We must get out of the city for a few days. We need to hide from Raúl and his men. They will continue to look for us and they know where I live. You are not safe. I am not safe now. I know of a place where we can go and no one will find us. My parents have a home in the north. Playa Somo. It's a nice quiet town. It is a long drive, about four hours. But they know my car. We can rent…"

"No. I want to find this Raúl and…"

Camila interjected, "David, we need time. We have to do this the right way. Evidence. We need time to think about everything very carefully. If Raúl is working for Valencian, then we need to find out who hired him and why they wanted to kill your wife. This is the closest we've been to catching Raul. It's not just your wife. It's all those other poor souls that Raul murdered. If we can build this case, then I can..."

David took a long, deep breath and conceded.

"Come, we are catching the metro back to the airport where we will rent a car. We can't go back for your things at my home. I have clothes at the apartmento en Somo. We can find some there for you too. Or we can run out and buy something. We need to get out of Madrid."

9.

Playa Somo, Cantabria 20, June, 16:30 p.m. CET

It was a long, boring and windy drive over arid, mountainous terrain. Brown, sandy hills with the occasional sparse plot of evergreen oaks, olive trees and pines, gave way to rocky peaks of monochromatic, sandy mountains. A minimal amount of billboards and barely any smaller towns dotted the landscape. There was not much to look at all, save for an occasional oversized cutout of a large black bull — the embodiment of Spain's collective attitude along the northbound A-1 highway. "Stupid," David thought to himself aloud, only garnering a cocked eyebrow from Camila. David had offered to drive but Camila saw the exhaustion on him and she declined his offer. For the first hour, they had watched the rear-view, certain they had been followed, but soon relaxed the search for a tail. David nursed his skinned knee and bruised hip with a first aid kid purchased at a roadside truck stop.

David and Camila had exchanged pleasant dialogue about their personal histories and David politely asked questions to continue the conversation but he eventually gave in and dozed off. His exhaustion overtook him and he began babbling incoherently as he fell into a deep slumber until they closed in on the northern state of Cantabria. He dreamed of Rebecca and being back in their home together, completely forgetting about the past 72 hours.

Camila nudged him awake as they neared the coastal mountainous region. David rubbed his eyes from his dream state. The trees turned to a noticeable lush shade of deep green, signifying the proximity of the ocean and a change in climate. It was stunning.

Descending from the mountain pass, the ocean came into view. It was an exhilarating sight for David and he regained his alertness. The fear they had both been sharing faded. As they passed the small coastal city of Santander, David took note of the sailboats in the harbor, the castle and lighthouse on the point, the unique layout of the hilly terrain and a sandy beach in the distance. They arrived through a winding road in the small fishing village of Pedreña in the middle of the large bay, which gave way to Playa Somo. It was a known retreat for British tourists and inland Spaniards, full of wide-open beaches, secluded coves, mariscos and surf culture. Not as quiet as David envisioned but certainly a welcome respite from the dry heat of Madrid. Looking back across the bay to Santander, David was reminded of San Francisco — it had a similar aesthetic, only slightly warmer and sunnier.

Arriving at Camila's parents' apartment, the view from the windows was picturesque. A harbor where the passenger ferry back to Santander came and went, and Santander's large buildings, and castle in the distance, were enchanting. The large mountains they had traversed earlier pierced the expanse above as they sat, watching over the coastal scene. It was hot today, but a breeze filled the home as Camila went around opening the windows. David took note of the lack of a central air conditioning system and began sweating. He perused the pictures on the walls of Camila as a young beach baby with her mother and father that mirrored the ones in her apartment in Madrid. The seemed to have a happy life. Her father was a pioneer of the local surf culture and was a respected waterman. There were a few of his vintage surfboards adorning the place. David recollected his youth — one filled with long beach days and surfing with *his* father.

"Your dad, a surfer? My father surfed as well..." David began.

Camila yawned, "Sí, yes, my father, he was a big surfer here. I am sorry, David, but I need a siesta. That drive always gets me sleepy. But let me get you some clothes first."

Camila disappeared momentarily and re-emerged with her arms full, "Here, here are some clothes. They are my father's … they should fit." It was a pair of sun-bleached blue jeans and a faded plain navy blue t-shirt.

"You go get some rest," David said.

"You should take a walk around, explore a little," Camila handed David a key, "Come and go as you would like."

"Okay, I'll probably go for a walk then and check the town out," David grabbed the key and put it in his pocket.

Camila retired and David changed. He plugged his phone in — it buzzed relentlessly upon its power restoration and connection to the home's wifi. There were at least a dozen voice messages and 37 texts. It was Rebecca's family.

David's tumultuous relationship with her father Cal, as he was affectionately referred to — short for Calvin, was a millionaire real estate developer who came from humble beginnings in the mountainous farmland in Northern Virginia. Amidst the Blue Ridge peaks and Shenandoah Valley, Cal forged his way from backbreaking labor on his family cattle farm to eventually getting into contracting, home building and developing. In his late 60s, Cal was a stern, blue-collar, humorless man that had earned his millions the hard way — laboring and building his own empire. David viewed Cal as a cantankerous redneck who found his wealth through unwavering bullying — an alpha male that knew his place in the world and played that role with authenticity. He despised David and believed him to be unfit for his precious Rebecca, which David regarded as partially understandable.

Cal hated sales people despite his reliance upon them in his real estate dealings — David's current career path had him in sales, something that David also hated. It didn't matter how much David loved and cared for Rebecca, it was about responsibility and providing for family — plain and simple — in Cal's eyes. Cal nearly refused to walk Rebecca down the aisle at the small wedding ceremony but was swayed by his pleading daughter.

In the Northern VA real estate development world, it's dog-eat-dog and there was no time for people who weren't hungry in the country's most competitive housing market. And that's precisely why Cal turned down Rebecca's idea of offering David a career with his firm. He regarded David as a do-nothing. David would've never taken it anyway.

The pair were cordial at the countless family events, holidays and vacations but David rarely escaped without a snide remark from Cal. David overlooked it enough to tolerate him, because he didn't have a family of his own anymore. He loved Rebecca's mother, Martha, however. She was kind, considerate, demure and loved David as her own. She exhibited a classical grace and elegant beauty that did not escape her daughter Rebecca's own appearance. She was especially enjoyable on vacation when she would have too many sangrias and let loose. Sangria was her favorite. She developed a taste for it in her college years while traveling in Spain as a young co-ed. Martha was the center of the family's connection to Spain and the brood collectively traveled there every summer once Cal became successful enough to afford to "spend the money before the tax man got it". Martha had indoctrinated Rebecca into a romantic myth of Spain, leaving Rebecca with a false dream of the country from a young age. Cal originally didn't care about where they went on vacation as long as he didn't have to work. Like David, he didn't particularly care for Spain and was begrudgingly dragged there year after year by Martha and Rebecca. He would've just assumed to go golfing for two weeks to perfect his awful swing.

Overwhelmed by the thought of having to share the news with Cal, David reluctantly made the inevitable, heartbreaking call sitting in Camila's family apartment. Just because he constantly felt slighted by the man and made him feel like he wasn't good enough for Rebecca, didn't mean that he, or any father, deserved this call.

David dialed Cal's number. The phone rang to a gruff answer, "Boy, you had better tell me what's going on. Where is my Rebecca? I been callin' ya'll. Rebecca won't answer anyone's call. Momma's worried sick."

"Cal. Cal, you had better sit down. Something has happened. It's ... it's Rebecca," David choked back his sobs, thinking he had better 'man up' as Cal referred to it.

"What? What ... what happened ... what happened to my Rebecca ... you ... you better tell me right now, son." Cal teetered between his temper and his sinking feeling.

"Cal, she ... she came to Madrid for a meeting and ... and they ... they called me ... the police ... they ... found her hanged. Cal, she's gone. I'm so sorry ... I couldn't protect her. They said they found her hanged in her hotel room. I know that's not what happened. I'm in Spain now."

"She's not dead ... she's just not. Boy, I don't know what has gotten into you but you better let me talk to Rebecca.

David, where ... where is..." The reality of knowing his daughter had passed into the beyond slowly crept in and Cal began to sob, David responded in kind — he knew how bad this hurt Cal.

"She's gone, Cal. They made her ... they hung her body ... they made it look ... like ... like a suicide. I came here to identify her body. There's been a detective here helping me figure it all out. I went to find out more from her company. And now ... now there are men after me."

Interjecting the sobbing after several minutes, "Cal. Cal listen to me. I am going to find who did this to Rebecca. I know I have failed you. I know I was never good enough for Rebecca in your eyes. But I swear ... I swear to you Cal ... I'm going to find them and make them pay."

It was the longest silence David had ever known while Cal collected himself. "David, you listen *to me*. If it's the last thing you ever do ... you find out whoever did this to her ... and you kill them. Do you understand me clearly, boy?"

"Yes sir."

"Good. I'll be on a flight tomorrow. Gonna take some time for Martha to come to grips with this."

Click. Silence.

After navigating the waves of emotion from the call with Cal, David asserted his belief that he would bring everyone responsible to their end. Cal's country justice mentality affirmed his purpose. He thought about Rebecca and how much it would hurt her to see her father like this. He needed to clear his head to start thinking things through. Maybe the ocean wouldn't be a bad place after all.

It took David a few minutes to make it to the beachfront by foot. He was buzzing with emotion that metastasized into vertigo. Finding a bench, he sat and watched the ground as legs of men, women, children and dogs traversed his periphery. Convalescing, he took deep breaths until he regained mindfulness. He continued towards the sea.

Welcome distractions engaged as he neared the village hub. As he turned down the last block before the oceanfront, the town came alive. It was a vibrant scene. Cafés, surf schools, teenagers running around in wetsuits carrying soft, foam, oversized surfboards, families, music in every direction, cigarette smoke, petite lap dogs freely pissing on the sidewalks, cheap beach stores and surf shops. Finally, the ocean. Walking up over the public access, there, the beautiful blue horizon greeted his red eyes. David watched the groomed aqua waves roll in like lines in corduroy from just beyond the small island with the lighthouse in the distance.

"Okay" David decidedly said aloud to himself, "let's go."

Briskly, David walked back to the now breezy and cool apartment, grabbed one of the vintage surfboards — a blue one — put on a pair of Camila's father's surf trunks and darted back to the beach. It had been a couple of years since David last surfed. He had loved it as a boy and young man, but the swelling crowds of the East Coast, the increasingly annoying culture around it and the patience needed for the right weather patterns to set up had caused David to grow impatient with it all.

It took no time to find his way back to the same spot he just checked — there was a spring in his step. David strolled between the topless sunbathing grandmothers, teens playing beach soccer and surf school beginners, trudging through the cumbersome deep sand. He could see that the waves seemed better up the beach. He walked to the massive bluff of sand and rock, topped with large pine trees that apexed at the center point of the beach where it curved inward. Just before paddling out, David stopped and looked around, assessing the scene: the small rock island with the lighthouse; a huge passenger ferry with the words 'Brittany Ferries' emblazoned on the side, navigating the narrow channel between the west end of the beach and the city of Santander on the other side; two additional lighthouses further in the distance as the headland reached for the bay of Biscay; and sailboats traversing the horizon. Santander looked beautiful in the golden light as the homes and buildings climbed over one another to be as close to the waterfront as possible. He battled with the thought of Rebecca and how much she would like it here and slowly made his way into the water. The water was clear and cool. The relieving wash of salt water rinsed the grime and grease from travel and David felt refreshed. Spain was tolerable all of a sudden.

Paddling out was tiring and his hip was sore from being tackled in the alley earlier in the day, but there were beautiful waves and the incredible view of the surrounding landscape only improved from the water. That massive sand dune appeared to be more like a cliff, about 80-feet high at its highest point — it anchored the center of the massive crescent beach and a small rock outcropping was where the waves focused and spilled their energy. David took his time and found a 6-foot, rolling, wave of glass. It was just like riding a bike and though it had been a while, David's muscle memory and physique embellished his technique. David kicked out of the ride and grinned ear-to-ear. It was a healing brine. For the first time, free from all of the trappings of relationships, stress, fear and anger, David found a window of contentment.

David surfed for several hours, losing himself completely in the waves. It was easy to do here in the summertime; it didn't get dark until 10:30 at night. David had already regained a rhythm with the waves, surfing like a young man again. Deciding it was time to make his way in, he noticed a familiar figure. Camila was sitting on the beach on a towel in a sweatshirt and shorts, revealing her bronze, shapely legs. Walking in, David's eyes caught hers. He was surprised to see her and that she had found him.

"It looked like you were enjoying yourself out there. You

are a great surfer; that was fun to watch ... my father would have been impressed," Camila gushed.

"How did you know where I was?"

"You told me that you grew up surfing during our drive ... recuerdas? When I woke up and you weren't there, I had a hunch that you might be out here ... also, your clothes were on the ground and one of my father's boards was missing. This was his favorite spot," said Camila.

"I ... I must've forgotten that when I dozed off in the car. Sorry about that. And, yeah, I grew up surfing. We have a great little beach town where I'm from, kind of the same almost — it caters to tourists, surf schools, overpriced coffee," David chuckled, then regretted doing so. "It's been a while. Rebecca didn't really care for it too much and I eventually gave up fighting for time to do it."

David looked at the ground in sadness but continued as to not embarrass Camila, "What time is it? I think I was out there for a while."

"It's 9:00. I'm sure you are hungry. I brought the clothes for you. You can rinse off up there — change and let's eat," Camila said, picking up on David's melancholy, gesturing to the public beach showers, in hopes of redirecting his mood.

"Great idea, I'm starving. Camila, this is an incredible place. The view is amazing," David stopped to soak in the awe of the beauty all around him.

The two worked their way past the still-topless grandmothers into the direction of the now-falling sun. By the time David was rinsed and changed, the sun was beginning to dip beneath the city of Santander — it was a magical sight — and the small beach town was beginning to stir again in the evening cool.

David carried the surfboard into the bustling café that

Camila had chosen. He was embarrassed for a moment but then relaxed when he saw that there were other surfboards leaning on the wall and on the ground. Camila, the warm and well-known local girl put her hand on David's shoulder re-assuring that he was welcome here. There were small children still playing outside, babies in prams, Euro tourists and Spaniards alike all partaking of the late evening "fresquito" and outdoor dining.

"So, you grew up here?" David asked taking a sip of the caña-sized Estrella brand beer the waiter had brought him.

"Well, eventually, yes. My mother was from the Basque region, and I was a small child there, but my father brought us here," Camila replied.

"Your English seems to have improved, by the way. Not that it needed it ... it's just clearer..."

"Yes, whenever I come back here it does that. I had to learn English as a child. My father started a surf shop to cater to the British tourists coming over from Santander wanting to learn to surf. That's it, right there," Camila pointed across the street to the busy and still-open surf store.

"He sold it to his manager when my mother..." Camila looked away.

David sensed that he should give her space to continue when she felt ready. He dipped the mediocre patatas into the attempt at "salsa brava", as she composed and continued.

"You see, not all tourists are good people on vacation. My mother was very beautiful, even as I was a teenager, I would be enamored with her beauty. But ... well, life hands you very ugly things sometimes. She was always so warm with everyone. The friendliest person you have ever met. Everyone loved her. She helped keep my father in business with her charm. She and my father eventually expanded the business to include rentals of small apartments for the tourists. It was all going very well until that one day. She took a group of traveling young British men to check in ... and ... well ... she never returned. We don't have much of a police presence here — it was even more remote back then."

Camila paused again.

"It took weeks before they found her body. It was buried high up in the sand dune, under the pines ... where you were surfing earlier. They had raped and killed my poor beautiful mother. My father ... my father was in agony. We knew it was those men and they had escaped on the ferry back to England before any formal charges were pressed. They were extradited back here but too much time had passed and the detectives did not do their jobs. They were released because there was not good enough evidence. Evidence, David. Not enough. That's why we need more evidence on Raúl." Camila said, attempting to shift the topic.

"And that's why you became a detective."

"Sí. My father went into depression, sold the business and went into the mountains. He couldn't bear to surf again, especially at his favorite spot where you were surfing earlier. He ... he had let those men do that to my mother; he blamed himself in that way. The waves were very good that day and he chose to go surfing as my mother checked them in alone. He was too trusting. After it happened, he said he could see her deceased soul wandering in the dunes up there from the water. He vowed to never return to the ocean. It was a very dark time for me and my father. We don't speak much anymore. He kept this home here for me. But, for me, it is a sad place. I haven't been back here in some time. I left for University on my eighteenth birthday for criminal justice studies. I attended a semester in California, abroad — then onto the police training school in Madrid. I buried my mind into becoming the best detective I could, to honor my mother. Sometimes I think her spirit is still in the apartment, twirling, singing songs, happy. That is my only comfort in keeping the apartment. It is for her, she loved it," Camila sipped her beer and curled her legs up into the cheap plastic and metal patio chair as the temperature dipped.

"Then … well, then, I stupidly got married to a man named Hector Morales. I was lonely and he paid attention to me — at first. I worked with him; he *was* a policeman. I say 'was' because he was fired for taking bribes. This happened after the first year of our marriage. He was also cheating on me, it turns out. We were only married for a year and a half. The divorce was final last December. I think he only married me … well, I don't want to talk about myself all night. It's your turn." Camila turned from her lamentation. "What about you, David?"

David's eyes grew wide. He drew a deep breath of the crisp air, then took a long slow sip of his cerveza.

"Whew. No one's asked me about my story, in well … ever. Wait — so you were married to another cop? What was that like? Seems like a bad idea to me … sorry, sorry, I'll mind my own business. My story then … hmm."

The earlier evening's ocean time, the setting, the view, the beautiful woman interested in him, the scene — all of it — drew him from his sullen dark recesses and mourning into a vulnerability he hadn't shared with anyone before. The emotional toll and distant thought of Camila as something more than a partner in solving his wife's murder got him talking.

"Nothing interesting, really. I grew up in a small beach town, not too dissimilar to Playa Somo, as I was saying. I was surfing with my dad by the time I could walk. I surfed as much as I could up until I got married. As a kid, I didn't concentrate too hard in school or care much about anything other than just being a kid and running wild, that is until my family — my mom and dad — were killed in a plane crash."

Camila's heart sank for him.

"They were coming home from a trip and I was at my

grandparents'. I was 12. I remember being mad at them for not taking me with them. It was their anniversary. They went to Saint Vincent in the Caribbean to visit my mom's family and were on a puddle jumper doing some island hopping. They hit some bad weather and went down. They never found them."

"I'm so sorry, David"

"No, don't be. Like you said, sometimes ugly things happen. I remember the call that night — I even thought to myself, as a little kid, 'good'. I was angry at them for not taking me and leaving me behind. But at the funeral that all changed. It shocked me to the core. I had never felt sadness like that. To know my parents's bodies were drifting out there in the ocean — lost forever. I was lost for a while after that, myself. Numb. Maybe I still am. My depression has kept me from really doing the things I wanted to since then."

The two took sips out of their beers and made eye contact. David continued.

"I think I developed the depression when I was a kid but I didn't know what it was or why I felt sad all the time. My grandfather just told me it was grief from my parents. But it was more than that. I put what little energy I had into school and getting into college but I wasn't a great student. I just barely got out a degree in Marine Biology — barely. My grandparents paid off my loans just before they both passed away. I just couldn't focus. I was aimless, restless. I had no one left. I traveled for a bit, wasting the rest of the little money they left behind. Turns out unless you are good at grant writing, Marine Biology is a tough career field. I finally left my little town in South Carolina because there was nothing there for me anymore and moved to Washington D.C. I took a stupid sales job after not making it as anything else. I found a little bit of success but couldn't really break through to where I wanted to be. I was what you might call a sad sack."

"Que es 'sad sack'?

"Ha, well, someone who just can't seem to do any good."

"I don't see that."

"Well, you might be the only one. Anyway, that's when Rebecca and I met. I had never even seen anyone like her, let alone known anyone like her. I was captivated. Her eyes. Green as an emerald."

David looked at Camila's empathetic expression.

"She was kind and sweet. She wasn't perfect, of course — neither was I — it's just that she didn't like the life I was in. She wanted to see me succeed. *And* she wanted to be away from the ocean. She was an urbanite. We gave each other everything we had. It was good … for a long time. Lately, though, things had changed. She was buried into her work … or … or disappointed in me. Either way, she found something else. I don't know. Now, she has been taken from me before I had a chance to …"

David looked up to avoid revealing the tears that had welled up. "I know that this isn't right. I owe it to her to fix this. To avenge her. I have to bring these bastards down. I just … I just don't know how. I get so angry that I can't think straight. I need to focus … to do this the right way, like you said."

Camila reached out and rubbed David's arm. He hadn't felt a sensitive touch like that from his wife in several months.

The two strolled back to the apartment with a deeper understanding of the consequences of not making exactly sure that they were methodical in bringing down Raúl and Valencian Bioscience. It was the understanding of one another that had grown that they both couldn't stop thinking about, however. Camila could see David reaching, trying to find a way out of his ravine. She knew he had hard choices ahead.

"Tomorrow, I'll take you across the bay to the city. We'll catch the ferry. I think you'll like it."

The two said their goodnights once they reentered the

apartment, both left wondering and hearts racing after they closed their respective doors.

The sun arose quickly and shone on the mountains in the distance, behind the beach. David had drank too much and was nursing a headache as he walked into the kitchen to pour a cup of already brewed coffee.

"American coffee, aye?"

"Yes, my father grew fond of it and ever since he bought that coffee maker. It's hard to find here, you have to go to the El Corte Ingles in Santander to get it. I have found myself leaning towards it too, lately. Es mas fuerte," Camila said and cartoonishly made a muscle bulge in her bicep, smiling. David laughed, enjoying the lightheartedness Camila was displaying. It was telling of her feelings towards him.

Camila was already dressed in shorts a sweater, white low top Converse and a scarf, umbrella in hand.

"You look like you're ready for any kind of weather."

"You have to be here. One minute it could be chilly and raining, the next, you'll be sweating."

"I'll get dressed then."

"You have about 15 minutes. That's when the next ferry leaves."

"Ferry? Okay, whatever you say, boss," David said flirtatiously, masking his own, deeper, growing feelings.

David and Camila exited the apartment and walked across the street to the ferry port where a crowd had already amassed. More babies in prams, British tourists, Spanish folks on their way to work, and more significantly, pilgrims hiking the Camino de Santiago de Compostella stood waiting. David wondered what all these people did in real life and how they could afford to go walking for months.

Playa Somo and Santander found themselves situated in heart of the coastal route that the pilgrims trekked. European and American hikers clumsily loaded their packs on board the ferry, adorned with modern conveniences like solar panels to charge their phones. They were the only demographic that could afford such a time-consuming departure from work. There were no guard rails or fences. The ferry simply pulled up to a set of concrete stairs that descended into the water. David reckoned that such a lax public transport system would never be allowed back in the U.S.

The diesel from the ferry wafted through the passengers as it rotated 180 degrees in the narrow, graffiti-laden port. It was about 20 minutes from port to port and the ride was free from dialogue due to the loud, diesel engine. It gave them both time to think and soak up the incredible vista. The blue bay was flanked with beauty. A natural sandbank with massive dunes, snowcapped mountain crests in the distance, sailboats and kitesurfers racing by, and the peninsula of Santander promising a wealth of culture. They pulled into port, the deckhand tied off the ferry with the massive rope to the equally massive cleat, and the passengers wasted no time filing off.

"Let me show you around," Camila said in a chipper mood. She was excited to show her new friend the city and the enthusiasm didn't escape David.

"Let's go. Where do we start?"

"We'll start at the castle and work our way back," Camila grabbed David's hand and her heart palpated.

Spaniards love their public transportation and Camila was no different. The two boarded a crowded bus and David was able to make out some of the scenic city along the water as they rode 10 minutes up the hill to the picturesque, modern Palacio de la Magdalena castle at the tip of the peninsula. A sweeping view from the top revealed the quaint Playa Somo and Loredo in the distance from where they came. Sailboats, ferries and cargo ships continued to traverse the mouth of the bay in symphony and tourists took in the accompanying sights, the busiest being the small enclosure on the opposite side of the point featuring penguins and seals.

"This was my escape as a girl. I would ride the ferry over and visit friends. Growing up over there, it's a small town. Everyone knows everything. When my mom was killed, I just wanted to get away. I could come over here and blend into the city, you know? I could stand up here and watch my small town over there like a snow globe," Camila's voice cracked amidst the vulnerability. She hadn't talked about her mother in some time but she felt at ease with David.

After a long walk up and back around the palace grounds, David listened intently about Camila's stories until food began to beckon, "This is beautiful," David politely mentioned, looking around, "I'm getting pretty hungry though."

Camila smiled, "Of course! Sometimes I forget to eat, sorry! Let's go back along the water. There are lots of tourist restaurants along the paseo there. They are expensive but have a nice view."

Cutting through the heart of the city back to the waterway, they traversed through angular, sharp cornered streets, passing all kinds of marisco restaurants, tapas bars and mom-and-pop convenience-style stores. Camila pointed each one out and remarked of the various, pointless significance in typical Spaniard fashion. The rise and fall of elevation and accompanying occasional stairs made no logical sense to David. He felt like he was in some fantastical, mythical maze. There were many bank buildings, a beautifully situated plaza and a large, old, multi-floored market — the Mercado de la Esperanza, selling percebes and a sense of the sea that provided its bounty here. It *did* remind him of San Francisco. Camila took him the long way round, coming back through a small children's park with a large carousel where children squealed in delight and accompanying, squeamish parents tried to stifle their sickness. The squeals faded as they strolled through the greenway back to the restaurants.

"Pizza! Oh my god, I would kill for some good, authentic Italian pizza right now," David exclaimed, pointing at the small, authentic, Italian pizza joint along the road.

"You are the visitor, whatever you want!"

The waiters took a while but it was worth the wait. David ate an entire pizza himself and downed two beers. Camila laughed watching David eat like a ravenous animal.

"This is an amazing view," he said sitting back after his engorging, looking over the passing cars back toward the port.

"Eh, David, Listen. I have some ideas I would like to eh, show you. I have been thinking about this Raúl and your wife's company. There has to be someone else. Someone coordinating things," Camila regretted shifting the conversation and bringing it up. She had been enjoying David's company. Hector had never even been to this part of the country with her and David was the first man she had been alone with in almost a year.

The pleasant mood took a sour turn. Up until this moment, David had begun to feel the same nervous feeling as if he were on a first date. He couldn't work out the emotions he was feeling, straddling the mourning of his wife and being in the company of an attractive woman in a beautiful setting. David paid the bill that had just arrived and stood up. It was late in the afternoon now.

"Let's get going," David sternly delivered.

The two didn't say much waiting in the line for the ferry or on the rumbling ride over the water back to Playa Somo. A few cold pleasantries and awkward silences. The seagulls flapped and squawked overhead. The smell of the low tide was off-putting. The sun began to set over the city and the orange made the small town glow. The warming of their relationship cooled as the sun faded.

No words were spoken getting off of the ferry and during the short walk back into Camila's family apartment.

"You know, I am actually getting very ... eh ... sleepy, David. Let's talk in the morning."

David went for a walk around town to get a last look at the waves and attempt to sort out what was happening with his feelings. One minute he was on the brink of madness, ready to kill everyone and the next he couldn't resit thinking of what it might feel like to kiss Camila's lips. He was careening out of control, unable to make sense of how he was supposed to feel. He decided that there was no hope in trying to control the crash.

Camila retired for the night and was fast asleep by the time David returned to the apartment. He brushed his teeth, wandered aimlessly around the room and decided to get into bed. David sat up in his guest bed staring at the grey colored concrete wall with his arms crossed. He pondered to no resolve until he fell asleep. He woke up in the same position.

It was foggy, overcast and cool the next morning when David opened his eyes to the harbor below through the guest room window. A street sweeper passed along and an occasional jogger bounced by in the morning mist. The little anchored fishing boats and dories swayed gently with the rising tide, purposelessly without captains or passengers. The guest room was cool and comfortable now despite the lack of AC. David smelled the American coffee. It appeared that Camila had been up for some time as he stretched and walked out to greet her. Her blonde-highlighted and brown tussled hair was up in a wild bun.

Camila had cleared the dining room table and set up a work station, printing out names and surveillance photos. Camila was investigating Raúl on her own time well before Rebecca's demise and had laid out her efforts onto the table for David to review. This was the best usage of her unused vacation time that she had accumulated. Now she could now concentrate her efforts after an early morning email to her captain informing him of her absence. The warm and intimate rapport had chilled since the overnight hours. David sullenly retreated to his former state, both regretting feeling an attraction to Camila and for having given those fleeting thoughts a space in his mind that should have been occupied with mourning.

David knew how to turn on cordiality regardless of his emotional status, "Well, this is impressive. How long have you been up?"

Camila hastily glanced up at David without acknowledging his inquiry, "Look, here. This is a photo of Raúl entering the hotel. The one I told you about. It's just a screen grab from the surveillance footage but it is timestamped. It's a big piece but it's not enough. We need to connect Raúl to Valencian Bioscience. We may need to prove that he was working for them if he was off the books. Tell me what you were saying about them."

David jumped in the hunt, "Well, first of all Rebecca had discovered that there were ... let's call them discrepancies ... in the reporting of a new cancer drug. Her company serviced Valencian Bioscience, they were the client and they were treated as if they could do no wrong. There were millions of dollars at stake but it when it comes to the FDA, you can't fudge the numbers, like, *at all*. And that's Rebecca's specialty — numbers. She was coming to Madrid to confront Ana, her counterpart at Valencian Bioscience. It came down to her but Richard, her CEO, had final say in the matter. Ana and Rebecca were always at odds but I believe there was a mutual work-ethic respect there. We need to talk to her. She can clear up their meeting and tell us what the issue was and why Rebecca was so infuriated about it all. And that's where things get sticky, at least in my mind. If Richard was pushing her to close this deal up, then he must've known that the numbers weren't real and that the statistical analysis data was faked. He would've known better. So ... for what, money? He is already so incredibly wealthy. It just doesn't make much sense for Richard to sacrifice his hard work building Parax to make a quick buck. They are an industry leader now. Why would he jeopardize his own company by fraudulently passing off this cancer drug from Valencian Bioscience as an acceptable treatment to the FDA? They'd figure it out eventually ... and of course, he would know that ... like I said, it doesn't make sense. I need some coffee," David acquiesced.

"Is this the man you speak of, Richard Blackwell?" Camila dropped a picture in front of David as he poured his cup.

The blood left David's face. It was in-fact Richard. The photo revealed Richard shaking hands with a one Raúl Garcia. David looked up in affirmation though he was outside of his body, ready to explode in his mind.

"Now how about this man, Ahmed Bahl?" Camila dropped another photo with Richard, this time with a Middle Eastern man about the same age as Richard.

"I've never seen this guy before ... but wait, what the hell is Richard doing with Raúl?"

"That's what we are going to discover, David. Your wife's co-worker ... Ana, she is the person we need to talk to. Ahmed is her boss. We have a team investigating Raul and taking some photos. We knew who Ahmed was but didn't know who the American businessman was that he met here in this photo. Now we do, thanks to you."

David punched the table, "I"m going to kill him!"

Camila, in an attempt to calm David's rage, "Come, let's talk this over again and then we will be on our way back to Madrid to find Ana and talk to her."

David's phone buzzed. He hoped it wasn't Rebecca's

Peter Viele

father again.

10.

Ana Esperanza was afraid for her life as the the warm breeze and pleasant sunshine glistened through the shady deciduous trees. She walked with speed and intent through the Parque Retiro, certain that she was being followed despite her best efforts to avoid attention. A child screamed and she jumped — it was only a spilled ice cream cone.

"Venga, Ana, get ahold of yourself, Ana," she said to herself under her breath.

Why were the Valencian Bioscience private security guards outside of her apartment this morning? Had they been following her since? They didn't know about her garage exit point, which she dutifully took as a precaution, but everything was in question now — she had to be extra careful. Did they know that she had left a message for David Harris, the husband of her deceased co-worker, Rebecca? She had spoken to HR about her grief and asked for his contact information; had they told Ahmed that she had asked for his contact information? The unending questions swirled and entangled her mind. She was quaking with anxiety as she found herself at the lake in the center of the park — the meeting place for the one person who may be able to help her. Too many questions concerning her safety lingered for her to wait patiently.

Ana texted her contact in-between two pillars of the greek-inspired semi-circle structure overlooking the lake that stood as the center point of the massive, majestic natural park in the heart of Madrid:

"I am at the lake now … waiting for you. Please make sure you are alone and that you are not followed. See you soon."

"Perdóneme, señora, pero ha llegado el momento de que usted…" ("pardon me ma'am but the time has come for you…") As Ana turned for the tap on the shoulder, fearful that it was one her assailants, she was greeted with a bizarre clown — a Chilean immigrant half-dressed in clown attire and half in dirty street clothes. He continued, "…tenga un animal en globo!" (…to have a balloon animal!")

Put off, Ana waved away the personal space invader that smelled horribly of body odor with a single index finger swaying back and forth, as was the customary Spanish non-verbal communication of "no". She turned away and attempted to shrug off the rude encounter, and the subsequent goose bumps, despite the eerie connotation.

David and Camila's drive back into Madrid was expeditious and full of anticipation. The only spoke about Ana the entire drive, leaving their feelings behind in Somo. As they were speaking about the case that early grey morning, Ana called David and said she had information and that she wanted to meet. The pair were gobsmacked and pondered the implications. What information did they even need from Ana — where do they start? They weren't prepared. But … she could possibly connect Raúl, Ahmed, Richard … and Rebecca … that much they believed. By the time they neared Madrid, the believed Ana had information on falsified data as a motive and, hopefully, concrete evidence on his corroboration with Raul.

As they sat in the car at the stoplight, now in Madrid and nearing the park, they discussed the case and drank their lukewarm café Americanos. They had to settle for the less desirable, non-American coffee from a gas station on their way back from Playa Somo that morning. They had decided to spend one more night in Playa Somo trying to understand all of the connections. Neither acknowledged the real reason they stayed — the connection *they* were feeling, despite them not admitting it to themselves. Their sojourn had distracted them from the realities they were about to face — and they wanted more time.

David's phone buzzed with a text of instructions and he looked down to respond. They had missed the tail that had picked them up as they rolled back into Madrid and it was too late. Instantly, explosions of glass and metal blew through their car. In a blinding t-bone smash on the driver's side, Camila and David's bodies went limp, thrashing back and forth, shards of glass sprayed them and their loose personal belongings went anti-gravitational for a split second. A half-drunken can of Kas — a regional carbonated lime-flavored soft drink — drenched their loose bodies in a sugary shower mixed with the rest of their cheap café Americanos, blood and shrapnel.

It took about five minutes for David to come to. He could hear people faintly yelling at him through the wreckage. Camila had been driving. They had no idea that the older silver Renault that sped into their driver-side door knew exactly who was in this car and had been following them through the city until the opportune moment presented itself. On-lookers walked to the scene apprehensively and in shock. David could barely make out the shapes of people hunched over, leering in. He turned to discover Camila's face in blood. The horrific vision jumpstarted his adrenaline. Her left leg had been wedged by her own door into the steering wheel from the impact.

"Camila! Can you hear me? Camila!"

"I ... I can't feel my leg ... please."

Camila faded back into unconsciousness. Blood pumped from the gash in her head with each of her heartbeats.

The adrenaline surged through his body. Scrambling his hands, he found a phone. It was his. Ripping at his seatbelt, he freed himself and pushed through his off-kilter passenger-side door of the car they rented from Madrid-Barajas Airport to avoid a tail on the way to Santander. That idea had failed. A crowd had gathered just as the other car managed to tear away from Camila's side, jolting the car, and Camila's limp body, again. The driver sped away but not before many pictures and video had been taken by the bystanders.

David ran around her side and tried to open the door — it was wrecked shut. Since there was no more glass in the window, David reached in and ripped a part of Camila's shirt and pressed it against her head wound.

"Help! Anyone?! Is anyone a doctor?"

A young man ran to his aid and said something in Spanish that David didn't understand. He relieved David of the pressure-holding duty on Camila's head.

David spoke gently and directly to Camila, "Camila ... Camila, we are going to get you out of here, you're going to be alright, help is coming."

As David stepped back and assessed the scene, he tried to make sense of what just happened and tried to calm his adrenaline. Spinning around in confusion, several of the witnesses began coming up to him and asked him to remain calm himself, to sit down, that help was on the way and that the police had been called. His mind began to clear.

"How did they know?" He wondered allowed, "How did they know we rented this car and it was us?!"

One of the bystanders, an American, approached David "I took a picture of the car and the guy inside who did this before he peeled off — here, take a look." 1598 FBF, early-2000s Renault, silver, not that great of condition, wreck notwithstanding. David zoomed in on the photo. A dark-haired younger Spaniard man, maybe 30, tall and fit, looked like he could be military or a cop with chiseled features and muscular arms. David's mind fixated on the man's picture momentarily before suddenly remembering what they were doing back in Madrid in the first place.

"Ana. Oh no." What was he going to do about Ana? He thought. He had to stay with Camila.

"Da ... David," Camila came to.

David ran back to her.

"Camila, I'm right here. Just stay calm, you are going to be okay."

"You have to go ... leave me ... you need to go meet Ana ... we ... we can't ... you can't miss this opportunity..." The ever-vigilant detective insisted despite her traumatic injuries and fading lucidity.

David furiously resisted her request, "Camila, NO! I am staying with you."

"David ... escucha me ... listen ... you must go, the police cannot find us together. We cannot trust anyone now. You must talk to Ana. You want to find out who killed your wife. This is the only way, please ... I will be ok ...Venga! Go!"

David reluctantly agreed but felt it was wrong to leave Camila like this.

"I can't leave you like this ..."

"You said the police have been called, help is on the way ... David, you must go ... NOW!"

David reluctantly obliged and pushed off of the disfigured car, giving Camila a parting glance — she nodded in affirmation — before turning and running from the wreckage in the direction of Parque Retiro. The crowd of onlookers swelled now and several good samaritans were working at freeing the wedged door. It was chaotic enough for David to slip away.

David's clothes, borrowed from Camila's father's wardrobe, were covered in debris, glass and a small smattering of blood. The cool white Oxford and sharp grey slacks now resembled more of a homeless man's garb. It didn't matter. Though mainly unharmed from the crash, David looked like a psychopath running through the streets of Madrid. A wild, mad man on the war path.

Vaguely, David began remembering the layout of the park and referred back to his phone for instructions from Ana as he made it through the entrance. He would still make the meeting on time. It wasn't as hot this afternoon. Children squealed and played raucously in the grassy fields, birds chirped, lovers embraced under the shady trees, heladerias bustled, doling out ice cream to both children and single, grown men, alike, and a lovely breeze fluttered the leaves. David's chaos did little to disrupt the ambiance.

Ana, having been perturbed for waiting past the meeting time, decided to give David five more minutes. Immediately as she made this decision, she saw a very distraught and disheveled man walking directly towards her. *'Is that blood?'* she thought.

"Ana?" David presumed, panting from his jaunt.

"David? Wha ... what happened to you?"

"I was just in an accident," attempting to skip the intrusive pleasantries to get to the point.

David continued, "Ana, please ... please tell me you can help me find out what happened to Rebecca. I have been through hell trying to put this together and I believe you can help me."

Ana's body language revealed her to be conciliatory and contrite. "Do ... do you need a doctor? You look awful."

"Let's find somewhere to sit ... I'm a little light-headed," David said, slowly coming down off of his adrenaline. His body began to feel the impact of the intentional wreck.

Finding a spot of grass in the back of the park, behind the lake and the Greco structure, they sat in the grass, appearing as old friends, only one having a grievous affliction. Nesting birds circled back and forth, buzzing by looking for breadcrumbs and leftovers from picnics.

"Are you okay? Are you hurt? What happened?" Ana cordially and empathetically inquired again.

"I'm okay, I don't want to get into it. I don't know how much time I have. There are some men after me but I don't know why. Please, please, Ana, can you tell me how this all happened and what is going on? What do you know? I have some information but I need to put it all together," David pleaded.

"You came to meet me with men after you? David, I am already in a lot of trouble. Those same men are coming after me too, you know? I'm putting myself in further jeopardy by being here and talking with you."

"Look, Ana it looks like we're both in this, and now we're in it together. We can help each other and get to the bottom of this. Please, my wife has been killed and I'm probably next. Can't you just help me to understand why?"

Yes, yes of course. I understand. Where ... where do I begin? I was so sorry to hear about Rebecca, David. I cared for her, you must understand that. I cannot imagine what you must be going through. You must be ... I don't know."

She paused and then obliged, exposing the subterfuge how Rebecca was coming to Madrid to meet with her and Ahmed about the latest findings.

"Well, I suppose I should tell you everything because — because Ahmed ... Richard, I think that they had something to do with all of this. I think I can help but I am afraid. I am being followed. I am afraid to go into work now. They have been listening to me, watching me ever since I asked our HR team about you and about Rebecca. It is hard to explain why they would do this, but I believe they might actually be involved."

"How so?" David's senses ignited.

"You see, Rebecca was the best at what she did. She managed to always get things done. She would appease Richard; I think she saw a father-figure in him. That may be why she worked so hard for him."

David was surprised to discover that Ana knew more about Rebecca than he realized and probably more than he himself knew about his own wife.

"Rebecca could make things happen. She was diligent and Richard knew that she would always come through — he preyed on her need for approval and everyone knew that. Ahmed is another story. Ahmed is a slave-driver. He abuses everyone and demands everyone to submit to his authority and to deliver without compromise. I know that Rebecca didn't always care for me but if she didn't, I can only hope that it was because I was at the direction of Ahmed. Rebecca had discovered that we were, em ... how do you say? Changing ... altering ... the data. I knew it was illegal but Ahmed made me do it. Please believe me."

"I do, I do ... please, go on."

"Phase IV clinical trials — it takes anywhere from five to 20 years to complete. Valencian did it in four. It's simply not possible. Especially with cancer. I had a feeling the numbers were off—" Camila paused, "No, I knew, and so did Rebecca. Valencian started working with Parax about two and a half years ago after going through maybe a dozen CROs. They didn't like our methods. Mira ... look, maybe you do not know this but ... Ahmed and Richard are very close friends and have been for a long time, long before Valencian and Parax. And things are not as they may seem on the surface. They studied at university together. And did you know, David, that Richard was a primary investor of Valencian? Of course nobody knows that, especially not the SEC. It's a completely illegal practice but at the time, the laws weren't as enforced and they were smart about covering their tracks. He gave Ahmed cash — under the table, and off the books, of course, to get Valencian going. That's the same time Parax got started. The only reason I know this is because Ahmed was drinking late one night in the office. He made me stay on. I overheard him talking to Richard. They have been close as long as I've known Ahmed."

David shifted his confounded expression to a cold, steely gaze across the trees of the park at the revelation.

"Nothing adds up anymore. We were hot in the beginning. Investors lined up like lambs to the slaughter with RXG1 and the results we were posting. It was insanity. Now, things seem like they are speeding towards a sale or some inevitable end that I don't know of. The SEC started calling this month — Ahmed got spooked. And with Rebecca nosing in and poking around deeper, he and Richard were pushed to do something about it to prevent themselves from being caught by someone on the inside. I believe that they have had this plan since the beginning — to defraud our investors. Our latest quarterly results that we submitted were, shall we say? Altered. That's what put it over the edge for me. I knew then that Ahmed and Richard had been angling some strategy to burn the company down and walk away at the end of all of this richer. They will stop at nothing from being exposed and having this drug get to market before they cash out. That has to be why this is all happening — there is no other explanation. I know that now because there was no way that she would let this happen —she must have discovered that some portion of all of this malfeasance. She was coming to Madrid because Richard and Ahmed orchestrated it. But, she found the tear in the veil. She knew. And they knew that she did. They must've been worried that she and I were going to put the pieces together. I'm sorry I am paranoid and to be the one to have to tell you all of this. I haven't slept, I haven't told anyone and I'm scared. I know too much. Do you see where I am going with this, David? I am in trouble for knowing that much already. Can you imagine what they would do to me if they knew I was talking to you? That they had Rebecca killed? I'm next if I am not careful." Ana was trembling and talking a mile a minute.

At a loss for any semblance of a response, David reached over and held Ana's hand. She's not what David had pictured despite having heard about Ana constantly over the last year and a half from Rebecca. It was the only thing David could muster after the wreck and these revelations. He knew that she and Rebecca had met in-person on multiple occasions and searched her eyes for a wistful glimpse of a memory of his deceased wife. She may have had a bit of Gitano in her — she had that stereotypical Gypsy vibe that David had always pictured Spanish women to look like. Iconic. Very dark black, flowing long hair, dark eyes, Roman-esque, semi-crooked nose, olive skin. Yet, her English was near perfect. He liked her candor and identified the abrupt nature that Rebecca had not cared for. She spoke her mind and was direct — David liked that attribute. But it was all too much to take in. His head was still ringing from the accident and he was deathly worried for Camila. His stomach was queasy and he had the feeling of vibrating, like he had too much coffee. It was his cell phone buzzing — an unknown number. It was best, he decided, to let this one go to voicemail.

"Where ... where do we even begin? I ... I don't know what to say. Thank you for telling me ... for telling me all of this. But, how do we do something about it?" As the words left this mouth a left turn overcame him — his clarity came into sharp focus. He had clear direction for his rage. It had now been catalyzed with this new information in a metaphysical chemical reaction. He knew precisely what he was going to do. And he didn't need an answer. Instead, he drew a question from the depth of his anger,

"Do you know someone named Raúl Garcia?"

"How do you know that name?"

"Do you know him?"

Recoiled, Ana apprehensively spilled. "He is private security for our company. But not really. He is a very dangerous man, David. Ahmed keeps he and Javier close and has them handle his unsavory business. Where did you hear that name?"

"It doesn't matter. I need you to tell me everything you know about Raúl. Where he lives would be a great start."

"Well, he's the one that has been following me. He would be watching us right now if I hadn't given him and his friend the slip leaving my apartment. He lives in La Latina — it's a little neighborhood on the other side of the city. Do you think...?"

Assured and focused, David replied, "I don't think — I know. And who is this Javier?"

David knew that Raúl killed his wife and that he did it at the direction of Richard, or Javier or Ahmed or all four of them. It was decided; he was going to kill them all.

"Javier Guaita. He is the the actual head of security for Valencian Bioscience. Raúl Garcia is one of his agents. Javier is also a Guardia Civil officer in the night ... eh, nightshift ... he has been there a long time. He operates from his home pueblo mostly ... a small pueblo outside of Valencia — Villargordo del Cabriel — but runs the security firm on the side for Ahmed most of the time. He's a bad man. If Raúl was, in-fact, the one who killed Rebecca, it was at the direction of Javier, who did it for Ahmed, or Richard."

"Ahmed. Where can I find him? Is he here in the city?"

"No, no, he took off this morning. He spends time in Valencia. That's where he and Richard are right now. At his apartment."

"Give me that address. I need to talk to them. I know you have it."

"Please, David, don't be foolish. This is dangerous."

"Give it to me."

"Fine. Here, I will SMS it to you," Ana conceded and sent David the address, "Happy now?"

Carrer de Sant Ramon, 2, 46003 València, Spain, buzzed David's phone and he stared at it like a homing beacon. David's renewed sense of purpose in finding these four men was no longer to prove anything. He didn't care about following the law or bringing them to justice. That ship had sailed when they tried to kill he and Camila. Nothing would prevent him now. He knew that he would kill them all, plain and simple. David wore the murderous plague on his face like a palsy patient — unmoved, transfixed. The dark circles under his eyes anchored the possession of death. Ana took note of his change.

Aware of his downward slide, Ana attempted to course-correct, "Our only hope now will be to contact the Ministerio de Justicia. The police are corrupted — Raúl worked for them and Javier still does, the Guardia Civil can't do anything, not if Javier is involved — they have a team of ex-cops. We have to go higher up. I have some documents and I recorded several meetings that I assisted Ahmed and Richard with. I think it's enough ..."

Blam! The unexpected gunshot sprayed additional blood on David's shirt. Ana's pulmonary blood suddenly poured out from the bullet hole in her heart. The horrified look on her face as she gasped her last breath matched the horrified look on the face of the teenage boy that stood over her now-dead body. The teenage street kid dropped the .38 caliber and started running in terror. David in utter shock and disbelief, tried the only thing he could muster — CPR on Ana. Nothing.

"Ana! Ana!" Still nothing. Her body had slumped into his

lap.

He slowly stood up and gently laid Ana's warm body onto the grass. Shock froze him in place. Not knowing if he should stay with Ana, chase the kid, or run himself, his head spun. Something stirred in him to run. Ana was clearly dead and of no further use, he rationalized — as cold and as harsh as that seemed — but if he was there when the cops showed up that would only implicate him. Or at the very least, slow him down. He thought of his options: Should he pick up the gun? Leave it? He had to get out of there, he knew. There wasn't anyone nearby — a few boats on the lake and a few strollers across the park, here and there — but everyone in the park had to have heard the shot. Surveillance cameras also had to be around somewhere too. Guns were not typical on the streets of Madrid. Only police and high level criminals usually possessed handguns and he wondered for a moment why a teenage kid had one.

He felt horrible leaving Ana there — it was the second woman in the matter of an hour now presumably dead in his presence. Fleeting thoughts came to David's mind about his involvement, his negligence. Not his problem anymore, David finally thought. Never had David been so callous — he had changed. His circumstances forced a fight or flight response mechanism, but something had gone wrong in the lab resulting in a Mr. Hyde persona that now fully consumed him.

'Enough,' he thought. "They're all dead," he said aloud to himself, thinking of Rebecca, Ana, and presumably Camila.

David began to run out of the park, avoiding groups of people, ducking behind trees, looking over his shoulder and attempting evasion from anyone, everyone. Madrid had never felt dangerous to him before — now it was a deathtrap. Horns beeped incessantly, the crowds of people walking around and going about their day and vendors peddling their ugly goods were hurried, louder. The noise was attacking him. Madrid had become a harsh war zone to David.

David looked like he had a mishap in a butcher shop and though appearance was the least of his concerns, he knew he had to do something about it as to not draw attention to himself. El Corte Ingles — like an oasis in the desert. Two birds, one stone, he rationalized. David pulled his phone out — now with only 50 percent battery — to route his best way to El Corte Ingles in order to procure a few items for his bloodthirsty endeavor, for which he was more mentally prepared for than ever. David remembered the mall-like store as having just about everything during all of his time here with Rebecca; legs of jamón curado, designer jeans, beach chairs, 10-gallon containers of olive oil, but more importantly, duct tape, knives, gloves, oh, and a clean shirt. A voicemail notification alert buzzed — he recalled the his phone buzzing earlier in the park with Ana. He looked at the phone as he walked down an alleyway adjacent to the store. He was reticent to play it, but did anyway:

"David, hi, this is Richard from Parax. "Gosh, I'm sorry I missed you. I would've much rather had this conversation in-person but I'm headed out of the city for a few days. Listen, I cannot express how deeply sad I am for you and for what happened to Rebecca. I cannot even … well, I am sorry, so, so sorry. I understand you are in Madrid. If you are still around, let's try to get together in a few days. If there is anything you need at all — anything, please do not hesitate to call me. I'm in Valencia until week's end. Talk soon."

Incensed with the David's nonchalant tone and the new notion that Rebecca had been killed for a money scheme, Richard's call only fanned the nefarious flame that had been birthed in David's heart. The sudden brutality inflicted on David's life capriciously directed him solely on revenge.

'Richard knew everything. He had to have known. He's playing head games now. Did he know I was meeting Ana in the park? How am I going to do all of this?' David momentarily feigned in his thoughts.

His primary intention now lay in distinguishing the light

in Raúl's eyes. He wanted to see it. To make him feel despair. He wanted them all to feel it. Richard would be last. One by one, he would climb up the snake's back until he could slice Richard's viperous head off. He would savor killing Richard. He hoped he could do it. With the grave reality of his intentions setting in, he had to focus more clearly and think about he was going to accomplish it all. He had to question Raúl ... to get him to talk, record it somehow, but mainly to get more information on how to find Javier, Ahmed and Richard when they were most vulnerable. David walked with intention, making it to the store in less than 10 minutes.

'To hell with Spain. Stupid little lapdogs pissing on the concrete, people blowing cigarette smoke in my face, and this idiot standing directly in my personal space,' David thought riding the escalator up to the 'hombres' section on the fourth floor of the major department store as a stranger rode behind him, violating his personal space. There was still glass in his hair, blood spray all over him, he had just seen two women violently killed and yet this jackass with his man-purse was standing right behind him on the escalator stair, literally breathing down his neck. David was about to boil over. Another leftover byproduct of the bygone socialist mentality, he deduced. Finally exiting his presence, David quickly paced off of the escalator defiantly huffing and stomping in the process as to send a message of annoyance to the oblivious rider.

David cooled and found the floor's 'Aseos' and washed his face and hands. Emerging fractionally refreshed, he assessed the range of styles and found a blue and white striped Oxford — a classic look, which seemed to be a preferred aesthetic amongst the more well-to-do, mature men here in Spain in the summer. He took the shirt into the dressing room, ripped the tag off, and changed into the clean, crisp cotton. Balling up his blood rag of a shirt, he stuffed it down his pants. He couldn't risk leaving it behind with the security cameras throughout the store. He took the tag to the nearest "caja" and paid an oblivious, overdressed male clerk who had no interest in David as he removed the security tag attached to the hem of the new shirt that David was wearing. It must've been a common experience for the clerk.

Darting around the ignorant shoppers, his mission gained momentum as he ticked items off of his mental checklist. He paid a quick visit to the perfumeria section and spritzed a sample of Dior all over his body. His next stop was home goods, third floor. Duct tape, presumably, would be ideal in taping up Raúl's hands and covering his mouth. He had never done this before — looking for kidnapping and murder accoutrements was brand new.

Carefully thinking things through was never David's strong suit. He felt more methodical than ever now, however. The malicious fever scratching at his frontal cortex tapped into the part David rarely used, thinking about every possible way to coerce a confession from Raúl, and then a plot to murder him to make it look like a break-in and botched robbery. That's all he could come up with amidst his buzzing mind.

Everything he needed on his malevolent shopping list was readily available. Home goods: Duct tape, a folding hunting knife, a generic, plain tan ball cap, a small bottle of ammonia, latex gloves — probably good to grab a couple of pairs, David thought. David mulled what else he needed. One of those stupid man purses that all the Spaniards carried around to carry said goods. Last stop: electronics for a voice recorder — *'don't forget the batteries'* David reminded himself.

David made his way to the next caja to check out with the remainder of his items and thought of Camila. He blotted it out. Instead, he stopped and grabbed the pack of cigarettes and lighter from the in-store Tabac on his way. He hadn't had a cigarette in eight years. Today felt right to pick it back up.

Barrio La Latina would be next. He remembered both Ana and Camila mentioning that Raúl also lived there and that he frequented a neighborhood bar called El Schotis. David stood daydreaming of watching, finding and killing Raúl.

"Bolsa para llevar?" The attended interrupted his dream.

"What? I don't speak Spanish. Speaka the English," David sarcastically and curtly replied, knowing full well what the overweight female attendant was asking.

"Would you like a bag for your items? They are .50 euros," the kind attendant replied.

"No just throw all of it in the bag I just bought," David felt mildly embarrassed by his intentional hurtfulness.

David walked out into the sunlight, lit his freshly procured cigarette, took a long, smooth drag and thought of Camila again. La Latina wasn't too far by foot. He knew exactly how to get there now.

By the time he walked through the city, the late afternoon hot sun had scorched David to an irritated state. He regretted the cigarette and threw the package with the remainder away. Having been in Barrio La Latina two days earlier with Camila, he had a grip on the lay of the land. He stopped in a café with a wide viewpoint in a small plaza across from a church and watched the front of Raúl's haunt. He sat for almost two hours until he was able to cool down in the shade. It was nearly 9 p.m. when he finally saw him. Raúl Garcia. He followed his routine like clockwork. He was bigger than David expected and he shook with a nervous fever. This urban creature of habit strolled in arrogant confidence to his favorite bar, El Schotis. David followed.

11.

Ahmed Bahl's austere and calculated persona always

intimidated anyone in his presence. That included the pleasant

ladies selling pastries in the street down below from his flat.

They feared him as he walked toward their stand. Going out for

pastries in the morning was his favorite thing to do and it made

him feel a slight shade of normal. The pastry ladies passed him

his goods and gave him austere stares. He retreated back to his

flat saddened by their lack of cordiality. He had forgotten that

he was an evil man.

His years on the streets of Karachi taught him the cheap cost of life and trusted that anything he wanted would be as simple as paying for it — including that small fee for Rebecca's life. He didn't think it was the wisest of plans, but Richard insisted it was the only way and that she knew too much. Ahmed was the alpha male in every room, except for when Richard was present.

Richard was his confidant for the better part of 20 years, having met on admissions day at UNC Chapel Hill. The fact was, Ahmed actually singled him out that day. Richard looked liked the stereotypical white, frat boy and Ahmed saw that as an opportunity to elevate his own profile. Richard had wanted nothing to do with this Indian's advances but quickly came to recognize a personality that would aid him. Richard had come to enjoy Ahmed's personality despite his initial, racist feelings about him. And Richard also came to know all of Ahmed's secrets in due time, including his salacious appetite for brutalizing young women to feed his monstrous needs. Like the time Ahmed killed a young coed in their dorm room when they were in their sophomore year. They were a peerless pairing and their fates would be inextricably linked forever.

Ahmed was good at coercing young women with his exotic looks, subtle accent and intelligence. This particular, unfortunate, young lady came to her untimely demise after meeting Ahmed at a fraternity party — one neither he nor Richard were a part of — and succumbing to his advances. She didn't want to have sex but Ahmed saw things differently, and when she refused, he choked the lights out of her young, beautiful, innocent brown eyes. Ahmed had a knack for being a little rough with girls but this was a new frontier. Ahmed didn't first intend on killing the girl, but as he saw her squirm for her life and held her fate in his hands, he could feel the rush of endorphins telling him to finish the job. It took longer than Ahmed anticipated as the the girl had more fight in her than he assumed. Finally, she gave her soul up. He stood over her naked body, staring for an eternity. Remorse immediately set in and he sat at her feet wondering what to do next.

Richard followed the etiquette rules of allowing a window of time after bringing a girl back to the room from the party. He wondered if Ahmed got lucky as he sauntered back to their shared dorm room, having struck out himself. The door still closed, sock still on the handle, Richard had nowhere else to retreat to and decided that enough time had elapsed for Ahmed to have had his fun. He loudly announced his intention to enter, unlocked the door and upon arrival, discovered the lifeless girl in Ahmed's bed, as he sat at the foot of it, slumped over, head in hands.

They buried the girl in the woods off of I-40 together. It was decided that after much deliberation that there was no other way. Ahmed convinced Richard that his life would be ruined too — he'd be an accomplice. Richard obliged his friend nervously but decided it would be best to get rid of the body. Richard shook through the whole messy ordeal. But something strange happened inside of Richard's heart that late evening: he discovered that he enjoyed the thrill of it all.

No one ever found the remains of the poor girl and after a six-month investigation by local police she was believed to have run away. She had vanished without a trace. There was no forensic evidence and no witnesses. She simply never came home from a party and every possible witness was too inebriated to provide any clues. In retrospect, the two recognized that it was an easy crime. The pair would walk past candlelight vigils and smirk to one another, savoring the fact that they were the only two people in the universe that knew of her fate. A perverse bond was forged.

Richard was a bored trust fund kid, who up until that point, had done nothing of any relevance or importance. He barely made the grades to get into the prestigious school in the first place, but his father lined a few pockets to ensure that his own namesake legacy continued. Ahmed was intoxicating to Richard. He was confident, dangerous and knew exactly what he was after in life. He had, effectively, set Richard's path and manipulated the willing subject to aid him in his quest for ultimate wealth.

Richard and Ahmed had become entrepreneurs during this period, proselytizing their well-to-do classmates to the benefits of illicit substances. It was a side hustle that started on a whim when Ahmed needed extra cash to pay for his tuition. Ahmed roped Richard into the operation. They became slowly successful at it and were smart about how they eluded authorities and narcs. Every campus party netted them more than an average minimum wage worker's monthly salary. It started small and grew to the point in which they had to make a decision to expand, or quit. It was then at that turning point that their shared business and economics classes introduced them to the world of pharmaceuticals.

After the first year of trafficking and making a fair living for two college kids, they decided to branch out and leave the street drug trade to the uneducated, lower class. They would start down a path that would earn them real money. They discovered the burgeoning world to be rife with cash and a market hungry for more — and it wasn't illegal. Deciding right there, in their dorm room, at the tender ages of 19 and 21, they would stake their claim and make a fortune. Then, they would burn it all down and walk away laughing. Ahmed was smart, Richard provided the initial capital and family connections. They were an effective team, understanding that importance of sharing the decision making.

Richard's father was impressed at his son's initiative to enroll in an unpaid internship at a Raleigh-based pharmaceutical Contract Research Organization. After a year, he was gainfully employed, rising through the ranks of the company as a Clinical Trial Assistant. Before too long, Richard's personality and interpersonal skills outpaced that work scope and he found his way as a hot, rising Clinical Research Associate. There he discovered how easy it was to play the pharmaceutical industry game — they were the ones who controlled the industry, he found. He had made his father proud, making it that much easier to ask he and his colleagues for money to invest in a couple of new companies when the time was ripe.

Ahmed chose to go the Biostatistician route. He was of Indian decent so the prejudiced white collar field pegged him as a natural mathematician and scientist. Richard convinced him that they had to play opposite sides of the field in order for their plan to work. Ahmed reluctantly fulfilled the role. Analyzing data wasn't the glamorous lifestyle he had envisioned himself living, but it justified the means to his desired end.

The plan was to develop a promising compound, deliver a proof of concept to multiple large pharma firms — of course with falsified data — and create a bidding war. The compound didn't matter but it had to be a hot disease. Cancer is what they decided could be the most lucrative.

Between the two of them, they soon understood how easy it was to falsify data and manipulate the entire system. Their careers took off. And, within a few years, both of their new companies were incorporated having gained funding from an initial capital investment from Richard's father. All of it was kept secret, particularly the funding aspect — a small loose end that Richard later tied up.

Ahmed was late getting back to his apartment after a fling with a young, wayward Norwegian backpacker. He looked for those natural blonde girls. They reminded him of the girl in his dorm all those years ago. Though this one managed to escape his clutches physically unharmed. The stop at the pastry stand had cost him a few minutes as he knew Richard was waiting for him back at the apartment. He was dreading this meeting with him and knew there was going to be difficult deliberation ahead regarding the state of affairs surrounding their recent clean-up efforts with Rebecca.

A hand reached him on the shoulder, preventing him from crossing the crosswalk that had been still flashing red as he stepped towards traffic in the direction of his home, "Your time has not yet come, friend," the pale, older Spaniard man, wearing a woolen driver cap and cashmere sweater.

A marisco delivery truck that had whipped around the corner unseen by Ahmed before his attempt to cross, now blew the pair back with a force of wind. He would have been killed instantly. Ahmed thanked the old man emphatically. Checking to see if all of his limbs were in tact, he spent a moment collecting his dignity before attempting to cross again.

Hastily entering his flat 10 minutes late, Ahmed saw a familiar figure waiting in the kitchen, preparing tea and coffee.

"Would you like some tea, Ahmed?"

Ahmed curiously raised an eyebrow as his longtime friend had grown more combatant as a business colleague in recent months, but he obliged the offer.

"Good, I'll make it for you," Richard confirmed as he took a sip of his café con leche.

Ahmed's cell phone buzzed as Richard returned five minutes later with Ahmed's tea kettle, cup and tray — he didn't spare any theatrical formality and knew Ahmed was a stickler for etiquette when it came to his British tea.

"Sí, entiendo," Ahmed said calmly to the caller as he hung up.

The pair sat down across from each other on the veranda in Ahmed's well-to-do flat, overlooking the Central Market where tourists fluttered in and out with their vegetables, fish, and baguettes.

"Javier?" Richard presumably asked.

"No. It was Hector. Javier hasn't responded to my calls. We have a problem, yet again. Something has to be done about

Raúl. He's gotten sloppy. Things have not gone according to plan and now they are spiraling out of control. This was your idea to handle Rebecca. I don't care about her but Raúl did not dispose of her well enough. You had better do something. I didn't come this far to have some two-bit hit man bring us down with his arrogance and sloppiness. Hector spotted David in La Latina last night but lost track of him and now he can't get ahold of Raúl" Ahmed lost his cool.

"RXG1 has gone according to plan, what are you so worried about? Rebecca is gone and no one else knows," Richard paused and reflected, "Don't you remember back in school? We knew there would be complications with this and that when it came to it, we had to handle this like a viper — be cunning, strike fast and show no mercy — those were your words. I helped you with your little problem — the girl — you started to unravel before it was my idea to get rid of the body, remember? Trust me. I can handle this too."

"Her husband, David, *remember*? How did he know to contact Ana in the first place? Rebecca must have told him something. No one else knew. That's why I decided to have Javier instruct Hector tail them. He flew all the way over here to identify her but ends up on the run. How does that make sense to you? Ever since he arrived in Madrid to identify Rebecca, I've had a bad feeling — and you didn't want to listen. He'd been with that lady cop for days. They ran when Javier's guys tried to grab them the other morning. Why would they run if they knew nothing? They knew something was up. When they got to back Madrid to meet Ana, I had to have them intercepted before they met her. Javier said she's a do-gooder and couldn't be bought. Then Javier put a team on them and hit their car. The cop is probably dead already but David made it out. This is starting to spiral, Richard. And I warned you not to bring up the girl at school again!"

"Yes, Ahmed, I am aware of everything that is happening.

Why do you think I called Javier myself to get one of his boys to clean up Ana as well?"

"Ana?! No! Not Ana. You didn't! She ... she was my helper. I needed her. Why did ..."

"Ahmed, this is almost finished. We don't need Ana anymore. She was just a worker bee. One of Javier's street kids shot her in the park in front of David. David is probably losing his mind and running back to the U.S. in fear as we speak. Everything is complete. It's okay. All we have to do is ride this out."

"I can't believe it has come to this. I am going to have a hard time losing Ana. She was good. And no, everything is not okay. David made it out and he knows something. Javier had the night shift last night so he's probably sleeping in. When he calls back I'm going to instruct him to find David. You're screwing all of this up and I'm going to have to fix your mess." Ahmed began to unravel from his position of intimidation — only Richard could do that to him. He paused in his frustration to take a bite of his pastry to calm himself.

"Don't worry about David either. I know how to handle him. I have an idea — the guy is a loser. I can make him think Rebecca had an affair with me and was broken up over it. I've met him multiple times. He's easily swayed. He's a fool. As for the rest of it, Ana was shot in a random act of violence and they got into a car accident. It's as simple as that. Don't overcomplicate things by overthinking. I can make him feel guilty for spending time with that woman after his wife's death. What were they doing together all that time? Consoling? Yeah right." Richard confidently quipped.

"Don't be stupid this time. You know what happens when you underestimate the enemy. I taught you that too. We wouldn't be where we are now — on the cusp of finishing our plan with RXG1 — if it weren't for *my* idea. I have shown you the way. Don't blow it all by being foolish yourself. We are about to walk away with millions," Ahmed said.

"Of course, my friend, of course. Don't worry. We're almost there. You know Javier is a pro — you found him, remember? He will take care of everything. You said it yourself that he's probably sleeping in and he is perfectly capable of any other loose ends. I will handle David when it comes time. He'll find me. He's that dumb and brazen to come into my den. He'll come, and I'll be ready for him," Richard calmly rebutted, watching as Ahmed sipped his poison-laced tea.

"You think you have this under con..." Ahmed gasped, then winced in pain as he clutched his chest. It was a heart medication that failed in Phase II, leaving patients with expanded blood vessels and, in larger doses, led to immediate cardiac arrest. Richard had kept a few vials of it stored in case a situation like this were to arise. It was not an easily procured compound — Richard had to manipulate several of Ahmed's subordinates to gain access to the lethal medicine.

Ahmed was attracting too much heat from the SEC and FDA and it was time to bring this decades-old friendship to its logical end. It was, after all, Richard's plan to get rid of Ahmed all along. Even in their college friendship days, Richard looked at Ahmed as a means to an end. To piss off his father, to make his own way, to gain respect for himself. He only tolerated Ahmed's pseudo-mystic, half-baked leadership principals and played the sycophant well until their businesses grew.

Ahmed, in the end, was nothing more than a street rat who got lucky and had a perverse penchant for hurting women — no doubt a psychological side-effect from his estranged prostitute mother. Ahmed's behavior took its toll on Richard's knack for playing the silver fox, Southern charmer. There were numerous encounters at the country club, the beach house, mixers and socialite events in which Ahmed's behavior towards women, though slyly played out by Ahmed, had embarrassed Richard. It began to jeopardize Richard's standing with his elite colleagues when they asked for Ahmed not to return to the next gathering. After all, Richard had been trained his whole life in the etiquette of the ruling class. Ahmed came from the streets and though Richard tried his best to train him for such outings, there was only so much he could do to curb his appetite.

"Well, I can see you are at a loss for words, so I am going for a stroll around the neighborhood. I'll leave you to it," Richard continued, as he picked up his coffee and left Ahmed grasping at his chest. The leftover flakes of pastry he had just consumed fluttered to the ground. Ahmed's body turned cold as his tea still gently steamed from his porcelain cup. Richard walked towards the door.

12.

David preceded up the stairs behind Raúl Garcia to his

is flat. Raúl knew someone was behind him, finally. He had felt

a presence tailing him for the last few blocks after leaving El

Schotis. He had a stalker and saw this man at the bar, watching

him, trying not to be noticed — he had failed.

David, finished putting his rubber gloves on and became adrenaline-charged with the thought of killing this bastard. He hammered up the last few stairs and slammed into the door seconds after Raúl Garcia shut it behind. He proceeded to pound wildly on the door.

Raúl yelled, "Quien esta ahí?"

"Policia!" David replied in terrible Spanish, with a hatred rising in his chest, simultaneously realizing that was the first time he had potentially cornered his wife's murderer.

Raúl shuffled behind the door, grabbing for some form of a weapon; his hands found nothing. Raúl was always on guard. He was a murdering sociopath. He looked over his shoulder everywhere he went. This time, however, he was unprepared for this confrontation.

David throwing his shoulder into the cheap door, then wedging his foot in enough to give him the leverage to get into the room, surprised Garcia … and himself. David's adrenaline pumped again; he always thought he would be capable of something like this, and he was about to find out if he was. Startled at the sudden confrontation, the men sized each other up as they were now face-to-face for the first time. David's fear took over and he immediately withdrew his plan for cold-blooded murder; maybe his interrogation plan would work.

"She worked for Parax; you know exactly who I'm talking…"

"I don't you or anything about your wife, I don't even know who you are. What makes you think I would tell you even I did know something?" He replied defiantly in his thick Madrileño accent.

"Rebecca Harris…"

Tackled at the waist before David could finish his sentence. Raúl began pummeling his ribs taking full advantage of David's obvious apprehensions. The last fight he was in was in the second grade against bully, Robert Palmer. Robert pushed the books off of David's desk and told him he was going to take his watch. The boys settled it on the basketball court, with matching bloody lips to take home to their mothers.

David reverted to survival mode. His hip still hurt from the other tackle by Raúl's man in the alley a few days earlier. He could almost see himself fighting this man from another room – an out of body experience. No, it was just a large mirror opposite him on the wall. Garcia's large, bear-like fist slamming the side of his head reminded him that he was still very much in his body. David's hands clamored for a solid object; it was a table lamp with a tacky shade that begged to be broken on his skull. The shattering of the lamp made more noise against his head than it doing any serious damage, but it gave David an opportunity to get to his feet. Raúl followed suit, returning to his wrestling pose. David lunged for him, tackling him by the neck. They fell through the wooden table behind them, which gave Raúl enough leverage to get on top of David again. Raúl, pounding David's face with his brute fists stopped only to begin strangling David. David's plan had spiraled out of control at an accelerated rate. Raúl eyes wide, smiled wildly, relishing in the blood sport. David began losing his breath and started to black out as Raúl shouted Spanish obscenities and laughing maniacally. David started to fade and thought he was dreaming when he saw a small penknife, about the size of a finger, lying on the ground. David never carried a knife until tonight; he thought they were for macho survivalists, wannabe militants, outdoor posers. But he wished he had the bigger one he had purchased earlier in this moment — it still laid dormant in his man purse. The pen knife would have to do. It was the same kind of knife that was found at his wife's murder scene, a Parax-logoed novelty gift they passed out with beer cozies, Frisbees and other pointless, branded, marketing accoutrements. At that moment, David knew that he had to kill Raúl Garcia. It was him or David. David used his last breath to reach for it and in one motion, unfolded and slashed his hand that was holding his face down. Raúl yelped.

David regained his vision and breath and decided to stab at him with the knife. As he cowered over his hand David slashed at Raúl, missing him. That couldn't happen again. In an effort to end things quickly, David went for the jugular, this time in a stabbing motion, that with Raúl's reactionary flailing lunge towards him, completed the job more thoroughly, slicing across his entire neck.

The violent exchange was over abruptly and suddenly. Blood erupted onto the floor and onto David's feet. The blood didn't seem real, not like the movies. David had never seen that much blood before. Garcia was dying, and quickly. Grasping at his throat as he collapsed to his knees, the blood oozing faster and faster, he choked on his words ... "Guaita ... Blackwell ... me enviaron ..."

David rushed for his bag that had fallen to the floor in the grapple and pulled out his roll of duct tape — the gun came with it, the one he picked up in the park, which he probably should have used in hindsight, he now thought. David got behind Raúl and duct-taped his massive wound, semi shut and used the opportunity to duct tape his fat, swollen hands behind his back. The massive undertaking to get him to a chair and duct tape his torso and legs to it was arduous and exhausting. Blood was all over the place now. It was a disastrous debacle. Raúl's moaning was obnoxious and annoying.

"Shut up."

"Ayuda me," Raúl eeked out desperately.

"First, you need to tell me everything," David clicked the recorder and began his interrogation.

"You killed my wife, Rebecca Harris, why?"

"Who?"

"Don't play games with me, I'm her husband," David reigned in his rage, knowing he was recording and tried to think on the fly how to better interrogate him.

The bleeding stopped. Raúl caught his breath. Raúl felt reenergized knowing that he could manipulate David's emotions and relished in the fact that he killed this man's wife.

"I do … I do remember her. She was quite pretty. It was a shame. But do you know what, my friend?" Raúl spit the blood from his mouth and paused, "It felt good. Very clean. I felt her last breath against my chest."

David picked up the duct tape roll and rapped Raúl across the face, nearly breaking his nose. He wanted to end it all and smash his face into a puddle but he had to restrain himself to get the information he needed before doing so.

"Puta madre!" Raúl regained his composure after groaning and yelling.

"Who put you up to it?"

Raúl finally, begrudgingly, succumbed to the pain, "Javier Guaita ... he's my boss. They ... they put him up to it. Javier gave me the instructions. He said it was to clean up a mess. I didn't ask questions. But, I know he was under a lot of pressure from the bosses."

"Javier Guaita. Where is he? Who are *his* bosses?"

"Villargordo del Cabriel. Near Valencia. He works the night shift for the pueblo police there. It's where he's from and keeps his family."

"Is he working tonight?"

"I don't ... I"

Slap! David smacked Raúl's fat, sweating head full of black hair with the duct tape roll again, juicing more blood out of his duct-taped neck. "Is he working tonight?"

"Ye ..."

The last blow was a little rougher than David intended and the lava flow of blood building up in Raúl's volcanic neck wound bubbled under the surface, then erupted again. Blood sprayed the room. He expired with one final gurgle as his head limped lifelessly to the side.

Standing over his lifeless body, David starred at the ground, unable to unfix his gaze on the lake of blood. Instinct, his only survival mechanism left in his tired, beaten body, took over. There was no way he could undo the violent chaos that had just unfolded. This was a crime scene. It was a scene of a horrific struggle. All David could do was stick to his plan of making it look like a break-in and robbery that he had originally devised before chickening out of straight-up homicide. He had to defend himself, he rationalized. So much for the recording — that would only implicate him in the murder. He would have to find Javier now and somehow repeat the process; he would need to think this one through this time.

He picked up the knife, ran into the kitchen, washed the blood off of his gloved-hands, grabbed some of Raúl's paper towels and the ammonia from his man purse. He wasn't sure if it would work but he had to try to remove any signature that he had been there. He wiped down everything, except for the places with blood and the broken lamp. Someone had to have heard the struggle but he remembered Camila and her murdered mother — evidence.

David, thankful for his most useful purchase — the latex gloves — rummaged through Raúl's unkempt drawers, searching everywhere. Nothing. Last chance. He checked his pockets. His wallet with no cash yielded something more egregious than he was prepared to handle. A card from Parax, reading: Richard Blackwell, CEO.

David, nearly unraveled, kept searching for more. He knew in the back of his mind that it was Richard all along but didn't want to deal with it. Now with suspicions and circumstantial evidence confirmed, there was no turning back.

David took Raúl's cell phone; rummaging further, he discovered in Raúl's front right pants pocket, his car keys to a Leon and a yellow envelope with 10 thousand Euros. David took them and put them in his bag. Giving one more passing glance through the room David threw Raúl's cash-less wallet, open on the ground with Richard's card exposed. Then something caught his eye. There, on Raúl's cork board of miscellaneous notes and flyers. It was Rebecca's Virginia Driver's License, in front of a small post-it-sized note: "Rebecca Harris, Flt. 749, American Airlines, 17 Junio, 6:30, Petit Palace Savoy Alfonso XII - €10,000!" Raúl, in his hubris, stole Rebecca's driver's license as a keepsake and was too lazy to throw the note he had written down from his employers about Rebecca. David couldn't believe it. He strategically placed the ID, note, Richard's card and empty envelope of cash, save for a few Euros — for added effect — on Raúl's counter to look as though they were casually strewn there. He would hope that whatever police detective came upon this scene would be smart enough to inspect these items with scrutiny but dumb enough not to connect David to the crime.

He ran down the stairs and made his way down the narrow street with his only possessions left in this world; a man purse with duct tape, a recorder with a now-worthless confession, nearly 10 thousand Euros, Raúl's cell phone and car keys, and more questions than when he started this horrifying journey — most pertinently, how would he find Raúl's car? Walking around the block, David clicked Raúl's keys incessantly until he could hear the corresponding chirping of his black Leon. David recognized the street — it was the same street Camila lived on. He had to be obtuse; as his mind drifted to her, he forced himself to think of Rebecca. David adjusted his new generic, tan hat lower over his eyes just in case anyone was watching him enter the vehicle. Nonchalantly, he drove off in the vehicle not knowing which direction he was facing.

After pulling over several times, from going around the wrong roundabouts, David finally had his coordinates entered into the GPS of his phone and made his way out of Madrid, again. He hoped the battery would last — he didn't have the mental wherewithal after his melee to stop at a gas station to find a charger. The Leon was unimpressive from the outside — it looked like a little 'grocery-go-getter' as he and his friends called station wagons as children. The manual transmission had some pickup, however, on the two-hour drive to Villargordo del Cabriel in search of Javier Guaita. Time was running out for him. Either the police or these henchmen were going to catch up with him sooner rather than later. There were too many dead people now and David was at the center of it, if someone out there was smart enough to connect him to it all.

David had a myriad of regretful thoughts and reassuring

rage-laced rebuttals at himself as he struggled to come to grips with what just happened in Madrid. He had pulled over just outside of the city to clean himself up — he couldn't have left any markers of blood in Raúl's car. The ammonia and Raúl's stolen paper towels came in handy again.

He had to think, to play every scenario out, which he failed — once again — to do with Raúl. His plan became clearer as the small village's lights illuminated the long dark road ahead in the now-pitch-black night sky. It was nearing the end of Noche de Las Bárbaras — the night of the witches. Upon arriving to the arid town, David found the local police station and walked through the dry night air, cicadas buzzing. He rehearsed his plan to act out the tourist-who-stayed-too-long routine for Javier Guaita one last time before entering the precinct. There was a lone young woman sitting at a desk in her uniform, smacking her gum and scrolling through her phone.

"Hello. I am a tourist from America. I got lost and I need help. I was told by my consulate to come here and ask for Javier Guaita."

13.

"**W**hat do you mean that won't due?" Javier inquired after the American had just confessed to killing a man in Madrid. David suddenly pulled out the concealed .38 he had picked up in the park after Ana Esperanza's brutal murder, and pointed it at Javier, the night shift Guardia Civil officer who had fallen for David's farcical confession.

"Face the wall!" David stood up and patted him down, removing his phone, which was concurrently receiving text messages from someone labeled 'Jefe'.

"Move!" David commanded. David had never held a handgun in his life until this day. He escorted the bewildered Javier to the front of the station after his pseudo-confession. Only the day before had Javier directed one of his team to smash into the rental car that David and Camila had been driving. He knew that David walked away but never got to see David's face, personally. They walked through the asbestos-painted grey walls and flickering overhead fluorescents to the front desk, where the receptionist remained absent. The underpaid 20-something was texting and smoking on the side of the building; she was oblivious to what was occurring and had planned to quit the next day.

The confession was a surprisingly cathartic exercise for

David, despite the elaborate embellishments, and it threw off Javier just long enough for David's plan to work. He was in control now.

Pointing Javier to his Guardia Civil-issued car, he put him in the front seat, sat himself in the rear passenger seat behind him and pointed the gun at his head, "Drive."

"Eh … Adonde vamos?" Javier took note of a familiar black Leon parked in the parking lot.

"Take me to your Jefe," David calmly jabbed.

"You want me to take you to my boss at La Guardia Civil? Vale, ok, por supuesto … perfecto amigo…"

David pistol-whipped the back of Javier's head just enough to jar him into submission from his insubordinate quip. He was more aware of his strength now after the death blow to Raúl, and knew he had to reign in his violence in order to get what he needed from Javier.

"Your other jefe … the one who hired you to kill my wife," David nearly losing his emotional control already knew the answer and needed to stay in control to get the answer from Javier on the tape. "My name is David Harris … not David Smith. You work for Valencian Bioscience on the side. You instructed Raúl to kill my wife. Who told you to do that? Tell me!"

Fully realizing who was now in his car, Javier took a moment, rubbing his fresh contusion, "Ay de me … joder …"

Javier thought quietly for a brief moment and decided to manipulate the situation by relishing his importance, "Ah … yes. You must be *the* David. You are tricky — giving me the wrong last name. We have been looking for you, well some of my men have been looking. I don't have time for fools like you. You're nothing to me. You know, I drove your wife the other day. Rebecca Harris, correcto? She was very beautiful. It was a pity." Javier calmly replied as he pulled out of the station's dusty road.

"Who?! Who instructed you?" David demanded, knowing the answer full well. David clicked 'Record' on his voice recorder that he purchased from El Corte Ingles. He would be careful this time.

Javier was a veteran. He was smart, methodical and maybe even considered by some as wise. He was a good 15 years older than David. David felt strange commanding such a seemingly gentlemanly-like character.

Javier sized up his predicament cautiously. This would only go one of two ways — either David was going to simply kill him, or he could take David to Richard and Ahmed in Valencia, which would buy him some opportunities to get the jump back on David. He decided to hope in the latter and would tell David exactly what he wanted to hear to keep him occupied for the hour-long drive into Valencia proper, where his employers would be. His abilities as an evasive driver coupled with his military background and propensity for bribe-taking are what attracted his moonlight employers in the first place. Driving this American dolt straight to them should be an easy task.

"You see, David, there are things in this world that are beyond our control. In fact, nothing is really, truly in our control. We are only here temporarily — me, you, your wife — all of us. We make choices to fill our lives with the things we want, then, before you know it, you are making sacrifices to your morals, your identity, to get those things. We are all on a path to destruction — it is inevitable. Rebecca — what did she want? What were those things that led her to Madrid in the first place? It was something, I tell you. *You?* What do you want out of this life, David? You made choices to be here right now, in my car, about to kill me. Me? Well, let's just say that I am like those things that are beyond your control. Like a force of nature. The wind blows, you cannot stop it. Now, you want to know what happened to Rebecca? Sure ... I will tell you."

David was mystified by Javier and his deep, gravel voice, "Go on, keep talking."

"Valencian Bioscience hired me to handle their security. I come from a background of making bad things disappear. Why a pharmaceutical company needs someone with my skills? That's none of my business — I don't care. But they are glad they have me now, I can tell you. I hired Raúl to handle some of the menial chores from time to time. Ahmed and Richard had a problem: your wife. She discovered something she wasn't supposed to, and, well, I instructed Raúl to take care of her. I should have done it myself. Raúl was a mistake — he was a murderer just for the hell of it. Thank you for cleaning that mess up for me, by the way — I suppose I owe you a debt of gratitude for that. That is, if you did indeed have the balls to kill him. Nothing can connect Valencian to us taking care of your wife now. My job is done. But don't worry my friend — we are all perpetuating toward oblivion. You, me, your wife, Richard, Ahmed. The end comes for all of us. Even your little police woman friend. What was her name? Camila? Yes, *Camila.* Her ex-husband, Hector works for me and helped take care of her today — how is that for poetic justice? He got to take care of his bitch ex-wife. You were lucky, my friend. But everyone's luck runs out," Javier paused.

"David, you are not cut out for all of this. You do not know the gate you have opened for yourself. Do yourself a favor and go back home and never come back to Spain."

David was taken back by Javier's grim candor.

"Just drive."

"I will take you to them, don't worry. They are in Valencia, at Ahmed's flat. He's a pijo ... a snob ... he likes the finer things — his flat is in a little district known as El Carmen. It is only an hour away. We will be there before you know it."

David looked at the address of Ahmed that Ana had texted to his phone earlier that day and mapped it by GPS to confirm they were headed in the right direction.

David stopped recording the conversation as they pulled up to a remote toll booth on the highway halfway into Valencia. La Guardia Civil vehicles are outfitted with the barcodes to be scanned as they pass through the more technologically sound toll roads. Here, however, all of the lanes funneled into cash lanes only — the scanners were down.

"I don't have any effectivo ... eh, cash," Javier informed David.

David passed a €10 to Javier and he passed it to the woman working the stall.

"No te preocupes, se hará pronto. (Don't worry, it will be done soon,)" the young pretty attendant informed Javier in Spanish.

Javier handed the €8.50 change to David and gazed curiously down the highway in response to the young woman's comment.

"Los escáneres están caídos debido a los incendios forestales. La red eléctrica de nuestro hub central se dañó y ninguno de los códigos de barras está escaneando correctamente, por lo que solo debemos cobrar en efectivo. Las reparaciones... se harán en breve. (The scanners are down due to the wildfires. Our central hub's power grid was damaged and none of the barcodes are scanning properly so we must charge cash only. The repairs ... they will be done soon.)"

"Ah, bueno, gracias chica," Javier smoothly replied, "Hasta logo."

They were still about 30 or so kilometers out from the city and they could see an orange hue flickering in the distant horizon. It wasn't the sun. The summer's wildfire season had commenced. The men looked quietly at the fire they were driving toward.

"When we get there, you keep your mouth shut, understand?" David commanded.

"Tengo que hacer pee-pee ... Eh, I have to piss."

"Fine. Pull over. No tricks or I'll blow your head off," David felt infantile in his attempt at an acerbic retort and shook his head quietly and to himself in embarrassment.

Javier pulled the car over to the side of the rocky road and into a deserted service road that led up to a mountain top that was closer to the flames. David was too tired to object and could also use a bathroom break himself.

A blanket of darkness surrounded the spot where they parked the car. It was still. The men exited the vehicle and David escorted them to the front of the car by the rock ledge facing them. The two stood back to back as Javier unzipped.

"You know, they are going to get away with it," Javier turned over his shoulder as he pretended to prepare to urinate and poke David as a distraction. "You ever hear of the saying, *'How dieth the wiseman? Same as the fool.'?*"

David ignored him but started to suspect Javier was stalling for some reason. Javier knew these mountains and hills intimately, they were his childhood playground.

"It is all meaningless. For all of us. Don't you know that? Your future is unknowable — it us unwritten — you have to decide how you are going to die though," Javier continued his esoteric ruminations.

David, still yawning, ignored the ribbing but couldn't avoid the rock coming down on his head that Javier slyly grabbed off of the nearby ledge and proceeded to smash over him. David saw stars and crumpled to his knees.

Javier had two choices — get the gun and finish the job or run. He decided to dive for the gun, overestimating the damage he caused to David's head. David vaguely made out Javier's dive in his peripheral and instinctually dove after him without a second thought. The two grappled through the dust and rocks, rolling over each other like lovers tangling between sheets, grunting at one another's advances. Javier was surprisingly strong in his older frame. Javier managed to get on top of David, as the two wrestled the gun at each other's fingertips.

POP! They both froze not knowing who received the gunshot. Slowly, Javier's now-white face looked down at the mortal wound in his heart. He got up to his feet, turned and began his waddling, tripping walk towards his boyhood escape. Javier made it about 30 yards, with David slowly trailing behind, until his heart stopped pumping blood to his feet and legs. Javier collapsed. David stood numb, looking at the older man's deceased frame.

David was no longer shocked nor horrified by the mortal terror he was a party to. His slow descent into numbness careened into deliberate malice. He sat down next to Javier and looked him over; his dead eyes open, the blood stream mixed with the dust and dirt. David crouched in the dust and surveyed the cold, dry land sprawling out from the mountainside. 'What am I going to do now?' He thought. He at least knew where to find Ahmed and Richard, or so he hoped. His newly acquired recording was probably not evidence enough; it would look like a forced confession. Maybe some of it would work, he hoped.

A dry breeze fluttered his eyelids. In the near distance, the wildfire lined the mountaintop, working its way down toward their position. Wildfires were common this time of year and were well managed. It was a part of life for the surrounding villagers, many of whom were volunteer firefighters. They understood that the fire would always come — it's how they prepared for and responded to it that mattered.

David pondered the second death at the work of his hands. He couldn't have dreamed to ever have been in this position. In an instant, the realization of Javier's words came into his mind. He pondered the truthfulness of Javier's absurdism and the rumination took hold. Despite his deceitful intention, David found the truthfulness of Javier's intention — ironic really, David thought. In a different realm, he would have liked to have spent time with Javier.

David lamented, standing there on the mountainside. He finally understood the uselessness of trying to make a safe life for he and Rebecca — it was never going to have happened anyway. Regardless of how he toiled, fixing their marriage, finding a career that would please her family, fighting his inner voice of depression — none of it mattered and none of his efforts bared fruit. It was always going to end up this way. None of it was in his control. His universe would always upend despite carefully laid plans and his establishment of order in every corner of his life. It was like a cruel joke that David wasn't in on until now, after the fact. *'Well, no longer'* David thought. Death and despair would befall him just as it did Rebecca. And Ana. And Raúl. And Javier. And ... Camila. All he could do was prepare for it, and choose to embrace the fire that came with it.

The surrounding craggy cliffs dove down like a behemoth in the throes of death, twisting, agonizingly until it met the rocks and jagged oblivion below. The nothingness threatened to swallow David if he misstepped on the edge. He took in his surroundings and his chest heaved with cool breaths until they slowed with a warming calm growing inside him. He liked the view from the rugged terrain and appreciated the natural beauty surrounding him. Now, no longer afraid and no longer angry — only embracing inevitability and the impermanence of all things in his world. The aching hurt of Rebecca being taken from him rose from his stomach and flushed his cheeks. David let out a roaring scream. The sense of isolation he felt, believing all who he loved were dead, gave way to careening, careless lawlessness. The previous paralyzing uncertainty in his life now replaced with an irrepressible dive into the ancient void — chaos was his new purpose. Order gave way to chaos.

His thoughts no longer listlessly floating in the air of his mind to grab — he was purely instinctual now, not needing such wasteful thoughts and pondering of his existence. David removed Javier's uniform and pulled the limp, naked corpse into a shallow ravine a few hundred feet away from its expiration point and covered it with rocks, dirt and sticks. If he would be found, it wouldn't be for a very long time.

David surveyed and inventoried the La Guardia Civil vehicle, finding a freshly dry cleaned uniform in the trunk, along with a police-issue shotgun, zip ties, a small shovel, extra diesel fuel for the vehicle, a lighter and a flashlight. Putting on the clean uniform felt like a violation to David, but Javier wouldn't need it any longer — they were close enough in size — it would work. David dug a small hole in the ground near the tree line. He placed the dead man's uniform and Camila's father's clothes in the hole in the ground, doused them with the diesel and lit them ablaze.

The clothes burned wildly and quickly with the fuel. The dry air that oxygenated the wildfires aided his as well. Then a thought captured David — burn the body. The wildfire would be a perfect cover for the death. Even though there was already a .45 caliber bullet lodged in Javier's chest, it would at least maybe help buy David enough time to complete his task and get out of the country. It was presumable that the fire would eventually make its way to their ridge in no time; the wind was on their side, and given his experiences in Spain so far, he knew that they would let the fire go until the last possible minute and something had to absolutely be done about it to mitigate loss to their olive and grape crops.

Carefully dragging the corpse out of the nook took more effort than David anticipated, especially attempting to not soil his new, clean uniform. There was plenty of fuel left and David poured the remainder onto the expired Javier. The exercise was grotesque to David but as the body burned, David took note that it smelled remarkably like grilled meat. David's cold, blue face illuminated, revealing the final metamorphic stage. David was a new creature. David was now an animal born of circumstance.

About 30 minutes later, the job was done. David was amazed by the amount of weight a body lost without its flesh as he dragged the charred, smoldering remains with a stick back to its cozy nook.

Closing the trunk after returning the fuel canister, there was one last thing to do — re-map his way to El Carmen in Valencia.

The last kilometers of road were deranging. The distant vineyards and olive farms off of the highway, slowly gave way to the pre-dawn city lights of Valencia that rose as he drove towards it. The arid, rocky mountainous foothills that had flanked the car on both sides throughout the drive had turned a slightly greener shade as he neared the coast. But it was a different green than the vivacious, vibrant green of the Northern part of Spain he had left only a day prior.

David was exhausted and yawned incessantly. David needed to rest. He found a truck stop just before entering the city and pulled over. He slept for two hours in the back seat, parked behind the building, wrinkling the dead man's neatly pressed uniform.

Groggy, he wiped the crust from his eyes and remembered the cash he earned from Raúl. Recalling his plan, he knew he would have to keep a low profile with the uniform and car — his Spanish was rusty and knew he wouldn't pass for a real Spaniard if he opened his mouth too much. He went inside the truck stop, made a coffee and handed the exact change to the attendant without uttering a word. Coins. *'Who still uses coins?'* David thought. The Euro's €1 and €2 coins were a source of annoyance for him and felt it was a completely useless waste of extra weight in his pocket. The coffee was awful, but provided the necessary caffeine fix to finish the day's work ahead.

It was a pleasant morning as David edged into town in the stolen police car. The sea breeze kissed the Moorish buildings. It was a very different city than Madrid. David patrolled through the streets of Valencia with his windows open, smelling the salt in the air until he navigated to the small district of El Carmen. It was littered with "artistic" graffiti. Interesting, but still graffiti, he thought. Paseo de la Pechina ushered him along the former Rio Turia — now Jardín del Turia — where the city converted a former river bed into a sprawling, lush citywide park. The bustling, hip district was alive and vibrant with the morning sun.

David parked the police car and decided to walk around as he worked out his plan. The sights and smells were exotic and a far cry from the regality and European Madrid, or even the North. It was warm, not hot, and humidity filled his lungs. The food smelled differently. The pastries looked different. The architecture resembled somewhere in the Middle East rather than in Europe. David nodded politely as people passing him on the sidewalks waved, nodded back, smiled and generally appreciated his police presence. It felt good to be seen and to be welcomed, despite the fact that he was an imposter. His skin complexion afforded him the look of someone Spanish, maybe Moroccan, and he blended into Javier's uniform. He liked his brief new role and even cracked a half-smile as he closed he took a panoramic pause and breathed the salty air in — Rebecca would've liked here too. He didn't mind it either. The distraction was short-lived.

David had only seen a few pictures of Ahmed and Javier gave him little to go on, other than the confirmation of his address. He couldn't just barge in like he did with Raúl. David would have to pay attention despite his brief daydream of living in Valencia as a policeman. And being groggy from the long, murderous night before wasn't helping him much either. It was now about 9 a.m.

David's phone alerted him to his dwindling battery percentage. Time was running out. He had no plan from here. David's heart palpitated from the anxiety knowing that he had no back-up, no alternative plan and a looming sense of dread for what fate awaited him once he actually came face-to-face with Richard and Ahmed. David recognized that he was probably going to die today. He thought about his own death and how it would happen. He then welcomed it.

Stopping in the middle of a sidewalk, David, all of a sudden, felt nothing. The nothingness engulfed him. No remorse, no happiness, no light, no heat, nor cold. Out-of-body, his mind felt suspended in mid-air with nothing to anchor it down. David looked down at his police costume and then his hand, puzzled, not feeling his own skin. He brought his eyes up to meet the eyes of a young boy staring at him. David attempted to smile. The boy only stared. His expressionless eyes pierced David's facade, and David took the arrow to his heart. There, now looking at him, were Javier's face and Raúl's face in this boy. The shapeshifter knew who David had decided to become. David's half-smile melted. He returned the blankness to the boy, standing there, alone in the sidewalk, statuesque. David awoke to remember all that he had done and the decisive action he had taken to now be standing there as a demon to this child. David embraced it. It was better than doing nothing as he had so many times before in his life. At least he was moving, deciding, no longer sitting in purgatory. He was an escapee.

David looked away as a passer-by brushed his shoulder, returning his eyes to find the boy vanished. David recognized that Javier had been a boy once, and so had Raúl. Innocent, beautiful children. And David sacrificed their lives, letting their blood on an altar of vengeance. Looking down at his fingers to find comfort in chewing at his nails, he stopped at once. It was in this instant that he decided to never chew at them again.

David felt the front of his police-issue uniform shirt to

make sure it was still there to hide his scales from the rest of the people walking around. He remembered that his seconds were ticking with ever-increasing speed and that his window was closing. He had to finish the job before his time was up.

Consulting the address that Ana gave him, he navigated to Ahmed's street looking at the nicer apartments above. A pastry stand enticed his olfactory nerves as he neared the block. He had arrived.

His stolen uniform granted him the front exterior door of Ahmed's building being held open for him by an unsuspecting resident. David found Raúl's door and could hear muffled voices. He retreated to the stairwell and weighed his options until he was sure of his plan. He was angry. And he was going to use that anger to overtake anyone and everyone in his path. He had a gun and he was in control now. He thought to break through the lock and bound into the door shooting whoever was in the room. He was ready to kill again and his adrenaline surged again, like it did in Madrid when he killed Raúl. David girded himself for the confrontation, putting his earlier wistful daydreams away and replacing it with the memory of Rebecca's demise.

Decidedly, he sprinted and motioned his shoulder to spear the door open but was met with a void. The door had opened from the inside, sending David flying onto the ground and into the interior of the apartment.

"Well ... hello, David," Richard cooly remarked at the flailing man.

"Richard! Wha.. What are you? I mean ... get your hands up ... where ... where's Ahmed?" David floundered from unexpectedly running into Richard, literally, and haphazardly pointed the gun at him.

"David, my friend, what are you doing in that uniform? A gun? What is going on?!"

David disoriented from Richard's presence rather than

from the miscalculated entry and subsequent fall quickly regained his composure, "Richard, where is Ahmed? Tell me what you are doing here, Richard!"

"I should ask you the same thing. Ahmed and I are colleagues. If you had called me back, you would have known that I was here. I'm happy to see you, but please tell me why you are pointing that gun at me," Richard authoritatively rebuked.

"I know everything Richard," David clicked the recorder in his uniform cargo pants side pocket and tried to calm himself, but the red in his face betrayed him.

"Look David, I don't ..."

"You can save it Richard. Rebecca. You were responsible. I know. I know you and Ahmed had Rebecca killed. I know you did. Javier, Raúl — I know you or Ahmed hired them. You took everything from me."

Richard perpetrated a dumbfounded facial expression, shaking his head.

David continued, "You and Ahmed ... you were cooking the books, faking that cancer drug to get it to the marketplace and fleece your investors somehow. What I don't understand is why you had to kill Rebecca. You had better start talking. This is the end of the line for you, so it's time for some conscious clearing. You owe me ... you took her from me," David's emotions rushed his words.

Richard weighed and measured David. He was unhinged and unpredictable, unlike in their previous, brief encounters in which Richard's cunning mastered the feeble David. This was a different man and he would have to adjust and throw everything at him long enough to distract the simpleton and make his escape.

Richard's face regained composure into a sly smile, "Well, you just have me all figured out then, don't you, my boy? Let's see, where shall I begin?"

David was spinning.

"I was never going to amount to much, David. You think because my parents were rich that things were handed to me, don't you? That's not the case — I had to make some very difficult decisions. Things that little people like you can't handle. You see, my father was going to cut me out. I had to grab life by the horns. And, at UNC I had the fortune of rooming with Ahmed and he taught me quite a few things about life. Things I would have never learned staying with a fraternity or at the country club. Ahmed came from nothing. He finagled his way to the U.S. and worked his way into school. I respected him for that and he showed me how to use that drive for my own life. We were angry young men. Ahmed wanted revenge on the world that took everything from him. Me? I just wanted power, my boy. We both had our own motives but we developed a deep appreciation for each other and swore we would never rely on anyone. That we would take everything that we wanted," Richard paused and took a long slow sip from his coffee before continuing.

"We started a ... shall we say, business at university. We were good at it. We found the pharmaceutical business almost by accident — we were able to procure some pharmaceutical ... *products* ... for our clients and thought, 'why not go straight to the source?' We knew we were smarter than most of the people in the industry. I convinced my father to bankroll my startup after my grades turned around — thanks to Ahmed — and before his unfortunate accident at his lake house. That was a messy business, I will spare you from the details but I had to get rid of that loose end. By the time I was able to, in turn, bankroll Ahmed getting Valencian Bioscience going, I was already netting a hefty profit. It was too easy. These people are morons, David. They want us to drug them and take their money. You're at least smart enough to see that, aren't you David?"

David repositioned the gun on Richard.

"It was a long game but we had an expiration date. We had to convince the FDA and SEC that things were legitimate enough before introducing our cancer treatment — all nonsense, of course. But I hired only the best people for our team ... that was my only mistake. Ahmed warned me about that: he warned me that Rebecca was too good for us. And, well, he's paying that price now for me," Richard motioned to Ahmed's slumped, lifeless body laying over the cafe table on the veranda. David walked toward it in disbelief, still pointing the gun at Richard. Richard smoothly turned positions and now had the front door to his back.

David was terrified by this calculating demon. He had met his match and knew that he would be bested.

Richard took David's presence as an opportunity to shift the narrative of Ahmed's death onto David's hands and manipulated the unwitting dullard further.

"And your wife? Ah, Rebecca was a peach. She really was. She tasted so sweet. It's the ones that are hardest to reach that always taste the best. And she gave herself to me. You always knew that she would, David. You see, son, women need men like me. And what did you have to offer her anyway? She was looking for an escape ... from you. She was so pure. Not with me though. I couldn't bear to do her in myself after our time together. Ahmed wanted me to do it myself, or not at all. Said I had to clean up my own mess. I just couldn't though. I had Javier have one of his goons handle it: Raúl. You already know that though, don't you?"

David stood frozen, again, as in life as he always had. The pain twisted in his heart. Unable to make a decision, unable to move, unable to respond, to scream, to cry. Until ... his hand moved, uncontrolled by his conscious. The force inside of him raised the gun once again and fired a bullet into Richard's soft flesh of his shoulder, missing his head. Richard winced and agonized but did not utter any additional taunts. He utilized David's confounding, catatonic gaze, as if hypnotized, to turn and run. Not the resulting distraction Richard was hoping for but it would have to do. Richard turned and ran out the front door, suffering a non-life-threatening bullet wound. David believed that he would never see or hear from Richard again. He stood with his eyes transfixed for several more moments, frustrated at his inability to kill Richard. His inner voice screaming at him to wake up. He shook his head, unlocking his eyes and rubbed them. Looking at Ahmed's dead body, his instinct alerted him to the impending imbroglio if he did not immediately remove himself from the apartment.

14.

David had to get out of Valencia. After deliberating his options in Ahmed's flat once Richard made his stealthy escape, David understood that he had nothing more than a tape, and three dead men, all partly responsible for his wife murder and that vengeance was not fully realized. Richard was gone and his cell phone no longer rang when David tried to call it, only a message that the line was no longer valid. David didn't touch anything in the apartment and after firing the gun, knowing that the cops would be there soon. He wiped the gun clean and placed it in Ahmed's dead hand.

David had escaped the posh apartment in Javier's stolen uniform, calmly removing articles of it as he walked down the street back toward his stolen police car. The cap in a trash can. The over shirt he removed in an alley and tossed in a dumpster. He was now only in a plain white t-shirt and olive-colored cargo pants. He hated the look of cargo pants but appreciated the utilitarian storage. It kept the 10,000 Euros from Raúl stashed and safe. When he went to approach the police vehicle that drove into the city, he noticed a couple of municipal police standing around it, wondering where its Civil Guardia operator might be. It became immediately apparent that the car was no longer a viable mode of transportation. That's when he decided that the train station would have to do.

Valéncia Nord was the main hub and was only a 15-minute walk from that alleyway. Turning a corner, the Portal de la Valldigna, an 11th century arched doorway that separated the Christian part of the city from the Muslim one at the time of its erection, met David as an imposing figure. David took it in. Acclimatized and numb to the violence, David was able to compartmentalize all that had transpired and admired the Moorish architecture prevalent throughout the city. He had never been to this part of the country and pondered the historical conflicts and conquerors that had besieged the city over the centuries. The Visigoths, The Moors, The Romans — they all came and went after their violent sprees. But where would *he* now go, David wondered.

David decided to get back to Madrid, make his way to Barajas and buy the first plane ticket out of the country with Raúl's cash. It was the only prudent option. He had no idea if there were cops or other henchmen on his trail. He took a seat on the train and tried to piece together an alibi story if it came to it. There was no one to give the tape to. No one to tell. If he did, it would only implicate him. Raúl was dead, Javier was dead, Ahmed was dead and Richard … Richard, the silver, cunning fox, disappeared over the ridge into the aether.

David sat down in his seat on the train and contemplated his next steps to get out of Spain. Then David remembered Camila. His mind was racing, but Camila kept catching up to the forefront. He would have to make a pit-stop — the Gregorio Marañón Hospital. He had to know. She was the only person that could corroborate his story and the only person on his mind. If Camila made it, she would be there. David had nearly sliced his thumb off trying to slice a tomato about three years back on a trip with Rebecca and had to pay a visit there himself as a patient. And, he knew that was the hospital they took in emergency triage situations. Uselessly waiting to be seen, thanks to the socialistic system, he saw numerous car accident patients being urgently wheeled through ahead of him.

By the time his train landed at the Atocha train station, he had it worked out — he would follow's Richard's lead and disappear. The inevitability of life's misfortunes would no longer be the catalyst for his anger. He was going to turn and walk away from it all. No more anger, no more frustration at the unfair things that landed in his lap. He had finally awoken to the idea that it happens to every living being on earth: death and misfortune. He was no different than the next man. He looked at the crippled young man in a wheelchair who had been sitting across from him the whole hour and 45-minute train ride exiting the train. He had smiled at David and had a kindness to his face. The young man was content despite his circumstances. He wasn't angry that he was disabled by some force beyond his control — he accepted his circumstances and moved on with his life. David smiled back at the young Spaniard and stopped blaming everyone else in his own life.

He caught a taxi to the hospital and soaked in the same familiar sights and smells of Madrid. The refreshing smell of Retiro Park's greenery, the handsome men in fine suits strolling to lunch, the pretty women, beautifully and classically dressed meeting them, the stylish architecture — he liked it, he liked it all. The chip on his shoulder was gone and his fresh eyes appreciated where he was. For the first time, he appreciated aspects of Spain, and Madrid. Maybe he even liked it a little. With the shroud of endless death in his recent life cast off, he was free to enjoy it.

The cab driver kept his car clean and cool and even made David laugh with his goofy jokes. He thanked David and held the door for him at the hospital. David walked into the main entrance hospital and up to the receptionist's desk to ask if a Camila Abaroa had been checked in. The pleasant and friendly receptionist happily gave him the unexpected good news. Room 127. Camila was there. She was alive. Thank God, David thought and his heart raced. David immediately gave up his plan to disappear when he walked in to see her sitting up and smiling back at him. His heart palpated. He had only known of her existence for a week now, but he felt an immediate kinship with her and protection over her.

"David!" Camila's eyes like a sunburst, greeted him excitedly.

"Oh my God. I'm so glad you are okay!" David ran to her and embraced the inspector, laying with her elevated leg.

"You ... you are okay too? I was so worried."

"Everything is fine, I am fine. What did they say? What's the damage here?" David asked, playing coy.

"Eh ... it's just a broken leg, a few cuts, a concussion. I will be alright though. What happened with Ana?"

"Well. That's a whole story. I don't even know where to start," David's fingers felt for the recorder in his cargo pants' pocket and silently contemplated the ramifications of trusting Camila with it. *'Can I really trust her?'* He thought.

"I know Ana is dead. I heard. What I want to know is, what happened?"

David conceded, "She was shot by some kid. Javier sent her. I panicked. I ran. After that I went to see if I could find Raúl and Javier."

Camila looked down and sighed, "Maybe your way was the right way. You trusted your instinct. I understand that the body of Raúl Garcia was found in his apartment. The detective on the case is my colleague — but I don't know if I can trust him. They discovered some incriminating evidence in Raúl's involvement of your wife's death. A payment, a note of some sort. As of right now, they have turned your wife's suicide over to a murder and have Raúl pegged as the assailant. Unfortunately, there is no way to prosecute him now, since he's dead. Tell me, David, did you have something to do with that? I won't be upset with you and you can trust me, what's done is done. He deserved everything he had coming to him."

David hung his head and stared at the floor with a slight nod of affirmation.

"Richard? Ahmed?"

"Richard killed Ahmed — he's dead. And ... and ... Richard got away."

David paused and looked at the floor in defeat, "Maybe one day, he'll get what he deserves. But ... I don't know, maybe he won't. Sometimes there are just bad people that can't be stopped. I tried ... I tried to... He won," David attempted to shrug off the loss like a seasoned, professional ballplayer.

"Look, there's something else I need to tell you. About was the accident that we had. The man who hit us. It ... it was Hector. Hector, your ex-husband."

Camila's face turned dour as she looked out her hospital room window toward the blue sky.

"Hector is a snake. I didn't think he would go this far though. How could he? How do you know it was Hector?"

"Javier ... he orchestrated it. All of it. When they were chasing us, the crash, everything. Hector works for him. Javier told me. It's all ... it's all right here."

Slowly, David revealed from his pocket, the tape recorder with the three conversations between he, Raúl, Javier and Richard on them. He decided to trust Camila and handed it to her.

"What's this?"

"Everything."

"David ... I ... whatever you did, I know why. It's okay. I am not going to say anything. The scales of justice balanced the way they needed to, as far as I am concerned. I will give this tape to my colleague — don't worry, I will say it was slipped to me anonymously. But ... Hector. I don't know what to do about him. I can't believe he would do this to me..."

Camila considered Hector, "Wait, yes I can. He's still out there. What is he going to do?"

"I don't know ... I don't. But I will be ready for him if he decides to come."

"I am so sorry about Rebecca," Camila said, her affinity for David growing deeper each moment.

"Like you said, things balanced the way they needed to. My only choice is how I react to these types of things. I realize now that I was angry for a long time, Camila. I'm not anymore. I hated the things that happened to me throughout my life I and blamed everyone else — it kept me compressed in my depression. I am not going to do that anymore. I don't know why I got pushed into this fire here. All I know is that I can't feel the depression anymore. I had to fight my way out of it, but I didn't know that before. I was misdirecting my frustrations."

David looked at Camila, "I will always love Rebecca, but we let each other down. We were dying together and we didn't even realize it. I am here now in this place though and there is nothing I can do to change what happened. I can only make decisions from here."

Camila looked into his eyes, affirming his new outlook.

"What are you going to do now?" She wantonly inquired.

"I haven't thought that far ahead. I'm going to take it one step at a time. Maybe I'll go back to Playa Somo. I liked it there. Besides, I need to replace your father's clothes," David replied, hinting at his budding desire.

Camila smiled. "Ah yes … yes, on that note. My father came to visit me earlier today. He has come back to life, as one would say. I guess my accident woke him up. We made up and he wants to be a part of my life again. I forgave him for leaving. Life is just too short to not appreciate the little bit of family I have left, you know?"

David's cell phone buzzed — it was Cal.

"Excuse me for a moment, I'll be right back." David walked out into the hall.

"Hello?"

"David. Where are you? I'm in Madrid. Took me a couple of days to get a flight over. I'm on my way to pick up Rebecca right now as soon as I get out of this damn airport. We are taking her home. I've been in touch with the folks at the morgue. Give me an update on your task."

"Cal, hi. Yeah, it's been … it's been hell. The job is done, sir. I'll come meet you. You tell me when and where."

"An hour, I'm still going through customs. At the coroner's office in an hour. See you soon."

Click.

Reconciling all that had happened, his need to see Rebecca off and the deaths he himself caused, framed against the hopefulness he felt with Camila, anxiety began its creep into his previously resolved psyche. There was a fork in David's road. Follow Rebecca and Cal home to D.C. and into a lifeless home that he didn't want? Or stay and choose the unknown path, chasing a faint glimmer of hope for a new life? It was almost a relapse into his former indecisiveness. Only David confronted it this time, head on. He wanted to stay. To be with Camila. That was it then. He'd fulfill his obligation with Cal and return to Camila. To what end, he didn't know. But he wanted to see where that road took him.

David returned to Camila's room solemnly but sure of his decision.

"That was Rebecca's father. He's here in Madrid now. I have to go meet him."

"I ... I understand."

"I will be back, I promise."

"Go ahead. You need to tend to her family. That is the most important thing right now."

David walked over to the bed, kissed Camila on the forehead and walked to the door. Turning back to her just as he was leaving the room. "You know ... all of this ... it was supposed to happen this way."

Camila smiled and David left.

It didn't take long for David to flag down a taxi driver — they circled the hospital, train stations and airport like sharks in an orchestrated shuffle. When prey was spotted, they pounced. As the most adept driver pulled up and exited, he recognized his face. It was the same driver that had picked him up at the airport.

"My old friend. You look much better today. Tell me. Where are you going?"

"The city morgue."

"Ah." The driver paused, took his hat off, rubbed his balding head and continued, "Pues, venga, vamos."

David got into the backseat and pondered what he would say to Cal. He was going to stay. Maybe start a new life in Spain. Hopefully with Camila. This trip changed David in every way possible, including his dislike for the country. At the very least, he wasn't going back home to Washington D.C. It never really was home anyway. He wasn't from there and had nothing to go back to. There were no friends — only Rebecca's sorority sisters and their dullard fraternity husbands. There was no family — only Rebecca's father and mother.

"Eh, señor … eh I suppose things are not … how do you say? Things are not so well … if I am taking you to the morgue."

"No, they're not … but they will get better."

"I like that, chico. That is optimism. That is a good thing, my friend."

The cab wound through the busy late morning streets. The large deciduous trees lining calmly swayed their branches over the Calle de Alfonso XII traffic and pedestrians, shimmering sunlight below. The hotel that Rebecca was murdered in only days earlier was in the distance. The car passed by as if nothing happened. David watched dutifully as the building faded from his eyes. He felt conflicted. He thought he should cry, but he didn't. Then he felt relieved.

"It's a beautiful day, no?" The friendly driver inquired.

"It is. It's a very beautiful day." David leaned back into the seat and crossed his arms with a sense of optimism for the first time in years. He was deciding to move forward.

The morgue was quiet. Cal stood tensely waiting as David pulled up in his taxi. David waved as he exited.

"Gracias, amigo," David said as he handed the driver his fare and closed the door — he was dreading this encounter.

Cal immediately walked directly into David's personal space — eyes red — and embraced the unwitting David. It was the first time since his own father passed away that Cal had embraced another man.

"This has been so hard, David. I know we have had our differences but I can only imagine how you must be feeling too."

David was stunned by the vulnerability from Cal — it was the first time he had ever witnessed any emotion out of his father-in-law. He could only reciprocate the emotion.

"It ... it has. Cal. I loved Rebecca with all of my heart. I am so sorry that this has happened. I tried to get the people involved ... I tried to make them to pay for what they did to Rebecca. I got ... I got most of them."

"What happened, David?"

"It was her company. The whole thing was a sham. She discovered some discrepancies and they had her killed. They had some plan to forge documents to get a cancer drug passed. There was an entire team of security guys. I ... I handled them ... but ... Richard, her boss. He got away. I'm sorry, Cal. I failed again."

"You didn't fail, son. No one would be able to handle that alone. Frankly, I'm impressed. C'mon. Enough of this now. We can talk about it later. Let's get Rebecca home."

The two men entered the grim, stark building and found their way to where Rebecca's cadaver had been laying for the last few days. Usually bodies are buried by now, as is the Spanish custom. The same round man who had been there when David first came, rolled Rebecca back out from her frozen tomb. Cal sobbed when he saw his lifeless daughter, only collecting himself to sign the certificado de defuncion with David, which David failed to do upon collapsing the first time at this sight.

Dead bodies lying in state always looked peaceful to David — as if the world can no longer harm them. All the cares, the worries, the pains, the challenging times — they were over and the deceased could rest forever now. Seeing Rebecca's embalmed corpse again was nonetheless jarring.

David had an epiphany standing there staring at his wife, "Cal ... Cal, what if we cremated her here and spread her ashes here in Spain. She loved this place more than anywhere. She belongs here. I think she would've wanted to stay here. What do you think?"

Cal stared off and pondered who is daughter was for a moment before responding, "You know? I think you might just be right."

Cal's eyes glassed over again. David patted him on the shoulder. "I think she we would be so happy to see the two of us talking. She will always be with us, Cal."

"Her mother wants her home. She's at the hotel right now. Couldn't bear to see our daughter like this. I'll talk to her. She might be okay with us splitting the ashes. I'll step outside to call her."

"Ok. I'll wait here with her."

Cal left David in the same cold room that had knocked David unconscious only several days prior. He wasn't shocked by seeing dead bodies anymore. Rebecca was looking less like herself after a few days in the mortuary. The Spanish officials were more than accommodating of keeping her around as the investigation unfolded and Rebecca's family traveled. Typically, they act posthaste in transferring bodies to the crematory or funeral parlor. Rebecca was given grace, however. David looked Rebecca over.

"My sweet Rebecca. I am so sorry. I wish ... I wish there was something I could've done to stop this. I wish I had known." David looked down then continued, "We never were going to make it, Rebecca. I'm sorry that I was too late. That I wasn't good enough for you. That I couldn't protect you. You are free from me now."

The coroner overhearing the monologue walked in behind David quietly and spoke softly in his best English to him, "Don't worry. She can hear you."

David was caught off-guard in his vulnerable moment with his wife's body. He looked at the coroner and nodded as the man patted him on the shoulder.

Cal returned 15 minutes later with an affirming look. "We'll split the ashes. Her mother agreed and that's all I need. I just spoke with the gal up front. They'll cremate her today."

"Okay then. I guess that's it. We can split the ashes here and I'll take her up to the sea in the north. She would've loved this spot that I'm thinking of."

"What's next for you, David? What are you going to do with yourself?"

David paused as they walked towards the door, "I honestly do not know. I think I might stick around Spain for a little while. I used to hate it here but somehow, despite all of this, it has grown on me."

The two men exited for the hallway that hardly passed for a waiting area, exchanging vapid pleasantries to pass the excruciating time that it took for them to burn Rebecca into ashes. David shared the details of all that transpired and how Richard Blackwell was the man behind the conspiracy. Cal was silent, storing the information in his mind. It was evident to David that Cal, despite the circumstances they were in, had finally accepted him. Cal's brokenness over his daughter had provided the vulnerability for the two men to mourn and heal together.

A couple of hours of awkwardness and coffee runs yielded two small jars. The two men shook hands with their portions of their beloved girl and walked together to exit the building. Cal hailed a taxi, David stood and stared into the sun.

Unnoticed by David, an innocuous passer by reached into his back pocket as the two men began walking on the sidewalk. The man had been surreptitiously watching for David's exit. By the time he had pulled the gun from behind his back, David had already grown keen of the expediting pace of the man toward he and Cal. There was a familiarity to the man that David couldn't quite place. David instinctually shoved Cal out of the way at the last second.

POW! The shot rang out and David's body hit the pavement. It was Hector, Camila's ex-husband who had rammed their car days earlier.

David's consciousness wained from the ground as he saw attending police officers who shared the same building space running toward the man and shouting at him. Cal was leaning over him, his voice shouting at him to stay awake slowly faded as David's eyes closed.

15.

Gregorio Marañón Hospital, Madrid, 28 June, 09:13 a.m. CET

Hector's moonlighting escapades surpassed Raúl's capabilities in the field. He was a quiet and diligent associate of Javier and Ahmed. At the direction of Richard, he had been tracking Raúl to ensure he completed the Rebecca task with efficacy all along. Raúl had come to Hector and Javier, knowing that they were working side jobs a couple of years prior. Hector and Javier were indiscreet about their side jobs from the Guardia Civil as security thugs. Though Hector's greed got him fired from the police, he was proficient in the private security trade. Formerly, and most notably, Hector had been working with a private equity firm that had some nefarious dealings with the Russian Bratva and had dissolved shortly before Valencian Bioscience came around inquiring about needing private security. Javier was the smooth-talking price negotiator while Hector had been the point man to collect assets for the team. Raúl was a reluctant pick-up as Hector was well aware of his temperament and penchants but after the Russians cleaned house with the private equity firm, equalizing half of their team in the process, Hector was desperate for muscle. The pay with Valencian was too good to pass up and even though the Bratva had put out a hit on Hector, his ambitions kept him from going underground.

The Russian Bratva would be Hector's undoing. Hector had been paid in advance and tasked with taking care of a banker who was set to expose the firm's illegitimacy, and thereby costing the Russians millions. He had failed to follow through, witnessing the banker with his small children. Hector didn't have the stomach to do it. The Russians knew that Hector was now working for Valencian Bioscience and they had been monitoring him. He had to be cleaned up. The Russians didn't care about the money; they were concerned with being misrepresented and their hired man not finishing his job. It was about integrity and reputation in their eyes.

Hector's decision to assassinate David in broad daylight did not come without great internal toil. He would surely be found out very quickly with plenty of witnesses and security cameras around the building. Or, he would simply be shot himself in the process. Both scenarios were a far better alternative to falling prey to the Russian team that had been following him for the last several days. They had come to collect. Hector rationalized that he could finish the job to net a huge payday from Richard who had called him during his flight to the Bahamas. Even if jail time followed, it would be safer than staying exposed on the street with the Russians watching his every move. Hector's play was to use the jilted ex-husband routine defense since Camila and David had been spending so much time together — that is if he was indeed caught. He had been watching her too.

Hector's plan came to a head when David exited the morgue that day. Hector was overwrought, disheveled, sweating profusely and wired on cocaine when he approached David.

His decision making skills had diminished with the chemicals coursing through his veins. His heart was beating rapidly as the shot rang out. It echoed in his ears so loudly that he couldn't hear the commands the officers were shouting at him with their weapons drawn. He turned and faced them and his body jolted and flopped like a rag doll with the multiple bullets entering and exiting his torso and face. He was dead instantly. Two Russian nationals with shaved heads and neck tattoos enjoyed the show from a black Range Rover with tinted windows a block away.

Camila Abaroa's crutches leaned against the window of the hospital room window as she sat, feet up on the end of David's bed. The cuts on her face were healing and the bruising had faded. Her knee was supported by a large, hinged brace. She smiled at David as his eyes creased opened for the first time in three days. He had been in an induced coma by the surgeon thanks to the gunshot to his chest perpetrated by the jilted hitman, Hector. He was lucky. The surgery lasted 10 hours and they were successful in removing the slug. Had it been any closer to his heart, he would've died right there on the sidewalk in front of the mortuary.

Camila had been released from the hospital the day before but decided to stay with David as he made his recovery.

"Where ... where am I? What happened?" David's eyes opened wider to see Camila waiting by his bedside.

"You went on a killing spree to avenge your wife's murder which was staged to look like a suicide by her company, and then you were shot by my ex," Camila wryly responded.

"Wha... how..." David was completely disoriented.

"Just relax, you've been in a coma for three days now. The surgeons were able to remove the bullet. You are safe now. You need to take it easy. I'm here and I'm not going anywhere," Camila reached over and clasped David's hand.

"Your in-laws. They have been here watching over you. I told them to take a break at the hotel. I gave them the names of some good restaurants to go eat something other than this terrible hospital food. They'll be back later this afternoon. They are nice people. I explained how you avenged Rebecca. Of course, I didn't tell them everything."

Camila grabbed her crutches and walked around the room to sit in the chair closest to David. She caressed his arm. David breathed her presence in contently. The two held hands for several minutes.

The television in David's room was set to the channel of the local news network. It seemed like Spain had caught on with the U.S.'s incessant need to run news all day long. That's when Richard appeared on the screen.

David's eyes widened and he sat up, "Turn it up ... the volume!"

Camila shuffled for the remote.

There, handcuffed in the front of his body, due to his arm being in a sling from when David shot him in the shoulder, was Richard being escorted to the police car. His head was pushed down into the back seat. His silver hair was disheveled and his face was scruffy. The Bahamian officer smiled wide at the press conference as he declared the collar to be a success of a collaborative effort between the Bahamas police force, Interpol and the United States' Federal Bureau of Investigation, in that order. Richard had absconded to his beachfront home in the Bahamas after the confrontation with David in Valencia. Little did he know, Interpol and the FBI had formed a joint task force and had been investigating Parax, Valencian and Richard.

Falsified data claims were reported to the SEC anonymously the day Ana was murdered. She had made a backup plan. 'Smart girl,' David thought. She had passed the information to another colleague outside of her company and told them to leak it to the press if something happened to her. When the newspaper, *El Diario* reported that she had been found shot in Parque Retiro, that colleague immediately filed the report with SEC by dropping the findings into the whistleblower function on the SEC's website from an encrypted virtual machine on the dark web.

Ana and Rebecca weren't the only ones who suspected misconduct. The lab's doctors and CRAs weren't all in on the conspiracy, and a couple of them decided to speak to the FDA and SEC months before based on various suspicions they were having about Parax and Valencian. Richard and Ahmed became too presumptuous of the loyalty of their team. It became an international case requiring a team of investigators to unravel all that Richard and Ahmed had done. Rebecca didn't get the chance for vindication, but it hadn't been in vain. Her murder, Ana's leak and David's tape recording all blew the lid off of the gambit.

Richard had gone straight to the airport and flew to the island where he been amassing a fortune in gold. It had always been part of Ahmed's plan to convert much of their earnings into gold. Richard took that idea from his now-dead friend and had been flying in gold to the island for the last two years on his private Cessna. With his hasty exit from Spain, agents on his case tracked him back to the Bahamas, where they had him arrested.

Once Ahmed's body was discovered by his maid, and Richard's prints were found both at the table and on the cup, the agents had enough evidence compiled for a warrant. Richard didn't get the time needed to clean up his presence at Ahmed's apartment when David showed up. The blood splattered on the wall from Richard's gunshot wound — perpetrated by David — presented the final DNA needed to place him at the scene. Ahmed clutching the gun, the angle of the gunshot, the blood, it all added up just enough to look like the two business partners were the only ones in the flat. The agents were unable to place who the man was wearing a police uniform seen entering the building that day on the apartment complex's CCTV security footage, however. He arrived and then left through the front door on the camera, but they couldn't make out his face and no DNA seemed to have been found that placed anyone else at the crime scene.

"I can't believe it. Richard, he didn't get away with it. Agh! My arm!" David winced as he pointed at the aberration on the television monitor above his feet.

The ticker below the replaying footage of Richard being escorted read: "Richard Blackwell, CEO of Parax out on $2 mill bail."

David's head dropped in defeat, and rubbed his face with his hands in disbelief at Richard's continued escape from justice.

Camila, conciliatory, "Pues, I ... I gave them your tape. I told them it was placed in my car. They have no idea who you were ... that is until you were shot collecting Rebecca's ashes. I did alter the tape a little ... I just cut out the parts where you speak — no offense. We're probably going to need to lay low though. They want to keep tabs on you. As soon as you are up for it, we're getting out of here."

"Wha ... what about Hector?"

"The policia ... my colleagues shot him. Shooting someone in front of a station like that? There were a hundred officers out front in a matter of seconds. Hector didn't even make it two steps. When they yelled for him to get down, he turned and pointed his gun at them. He was dead instantly."

"I'm sorry I caused all of this. I'm sorry about your ex," David said rubbing his slumbering eyelids.

"David, don't be. He was a bad man. And you? You are a good man. You are brave. You didn't think twice to get to the bottom of this. To push your father-in-law out of harm's way. To go after those men. Do not make the mistake of believing that any of this was your fault."

"I suppose then, I should thank you. For believing in me."

Camila rubbed David's hand as he jostled in the hospital bed, rediscovering the feeling in his body from being under for so long.

"Listen, I was dreaming ... for a long time ... in my coma, I guess ... that I was in a sailboat and there was someone on it with me but their face was blank. What do you think that means?"

Camila surveyed David's eyes, "I think it means that your future is whatever you want it to be."

"Maybe you're right. Maybe this is me starting over."

"Want to hear something funny? Hector had a sailboat. He kept it at a marina in Valencia. I know where his keys are."

David looked at Camila and smiled.

"I think you need a little more rest."

David's eyes closed and he felt a warmth knowing that Camila was there watching over him as he slept for the next several hours.

Cal returned later that night and excused Camila's post. David sat up and the two men talked. Cal said his final goodbyes to David, leaving Rebecca's urn on his nightstand. David believed it would be the last time he would see the man and expressed his sorrow for the loss of Rebecca again.

"All things happen for a reason, David. You take care of yourself. I only wish you the best, son." Cal closed the door and walked out of David's life forever.

David stared blankly at the nondescript urn with half of his wife's ashes.

Camila returned to the room after Cal's departure.

"The police are here to take a final statement from you about your wound. I don't think they'll have many questions considering half of the office saw it happen. But you should still be careful of what you say. I'm only telling you that as … as a friend,"

David agreed and two men in suits entered the room as Camila exited. She smiled to the two familiar men and said hello — they did not acknowledge her.

"Señor Harris. My name is Deputy Inspector Aguirre. I spoke with the doctors and you are ready to be released. But, señor, we did have some final questions for you. The man who shot you, Hector, he was formerly one of our own. Señor Harris, how did you know Hector?"

"I've never seen the man before. I was there collecting my wife's ashes with my father-in-law."

"Yes, we spoke with Cal earlier this morning. He said your wife, his daughter, had been murdered and that you had been in Madrid for a few days after. We are aware of the ongoing investigation and understand that Inspector Abaroa's petition to change the cause of death from suicide to homicide was successful. A Raúl Garcia was the perpetrator. Our team analyzed the note she left and were able to determine both that it was not her handwriting, when compared to samples provided by Parax, and that Raúl's handwriting matched the letters on the note. Further, DNA was, in-fact, found on the note — there was a drop of sweat." The detectives looked at one another as David put his hands over his mouth.

"We are very sorry for your loss Señor Harris."

The second man said nothing and only stared at David.

"Thank you."

"But, back to Hector, Señor Harris, tell me. Did you know

that he was formerly married to Inspector Abaroa?"

"She did inform me, yes," David cooly replied.

"And, you don't think that's ... how do you say? Peculiar? The man who tried to kill you was the ex-wife of the woman investigating your wife's murder."

"Of course. All of this is peculiar. My wife was murdered and it was staged to look like a suicide. A man shot me yesterday. And now there are cops questioning me. My wife worked in the pharmaceutical industry and I'm a salesman. We are boring people. I don't know why all of this is going on."

"I am curious. Tell me, Señor Harris, what have you been up to these past few days here in Madrid? It seems odd that you have been here for as long as you have. Your wife's body was in our morgue for much longer than they usually are. Why hadn't you claimed her body sooner?" Aguirre's line of questioning had quickly become more direct and his body language indicated a hint of frustration.

"Look. I don't know what you want from me. I think it's time that either I go home or I get a lawyer."

"Señor Harris. Did you know a one Ana Esperanza? She worked with your wife. She was found dead three days ago in Parque Retiro."

"I am sorry to hear about that. I never knew her but yes, I was aware that my wife worked with her. Again, what do you need from me?"

"And, Señor Harris. Raúl Garcia, the man we now know who murdered your wife — thanks to Inspector Abaroa — was also found murdered in his apartment."

"Good," David in defiant sarcasm replied.

"You do understand that you are the only living connection between these people, Señor Harris. We are simply trying to reconcile all of the events in the last few days. To understand the timeline better. We appreciate your cooperation in this matter, Señor Harris."

"Here's what you need to know. I flew over to identify my wife's body. I hit my head in the morgue. Your mortician can attest to that. I took a couple of days to recover and just grieve. I mostly sat in the hotel and cried. Is that what you want to hear?"

"And what hotel was this, Señor Harris? We just need to verify it for our records."

David's heart sank as he recalled the hotel he booked on his way to Madrid and that he never step foot in. "Uh, the Courtyard Marriott Princesa near the Museo de Arte Contemporáneo."

"Alright. Well, Señor Harris, we will verify this and we will be in touch. But please, do not leave the city until we can talk again. Could you come by my office tomorrow, at, let's say 9?"

"I suppose. I really would like to get the next flight home but sure, anything to help with your investigation. I'll be there."

"Thank you, Señor Harris."

The two men in suits exited David's hospital room. The one who didn't speak, looked over his shoulder and leered at David in his vulnerable gown and bed as he exited.

Camila hastily returned to the room moments later, looking like she was ready to leave. The attending physician entered behind Camila and after giving him some wound care instructions, handed him some paperwork to sign and officially released David. Camila and David said nothing until the physician left and picked up where they left off.

The television still on, played footage of a raging wildfire near Valencia that had grown out of control. David only stared, saying nothing, not acknowledging Camila. His misdeeds could soon be found out, though it was safe to assume that Javier's body was further incinerated at this point.

"David, what are you staring at? The fires? They are crazy, I know."

"Yeah, crazy," David robotically replied.

"David. Those detectives. They are trustworthy, good men, but … they know something that I don't. Something is up. David … I am concerned for your safety."

"I trust your instinct. What are we going to do, then?"

"I think we had better get you out of here."

"That's all I need to hear. So … what's the plan? Where do we go?"

"I thought about going back to Somo to to rest and re-cover there. You are welcome to ride with me. You can use my father's surfboards as much as you want … even stay with me for as long as you'd like. Of course, we could also go to Valencia to see about Hector's sailboat. I know where the keys are. And maybe it's better that you and I get out of Spain for a little while. At least until this case settles down. So … are you going to join me?" Camila gazed at David ardently.

David smiled, "I'd like that very much."

The End.

Made in the USA
Columbia, SC
13 December 2019